Why Casey Had to Die

Why Casey Had to Die

A Harry Bronson Mystery

L. C. Hayden

Five Star • Waterville, Maine

First Edition
First Printing: December 2006

Published in 2006 in conjunction with Tekno Books and Ed Gorman.

Set in 11 pt. Plantin by Christina S. Huff.

Printed in the United States on permanent paper.

Library of Congress Cataloging-in-Publication Data

Hayden, L. C.
  Why Casey had to die : a Harry Bronson mystery / L.C. Hayden. —1st ed.
      p. cm.
    ISBN 1-59414-493-1 (hc : alk. paper)
    I. Title.
  PS3558.A82875W47 2006
  813′.54—dc22   2006005602

If friendship is a treasure, then indeed I'm wealthy.

To the Porters—
in El Paso:
"Gene" and Kathy Porter
in Arkansas:
Dan and Linda Horton
And a special dedication to
Mama Myers

Acknowledgments

I would like to thank those who honored me by allowing me to name one of my characters after him/her. My hat goes off to Gerri Balter, Michael Hoover, Sammy Ryan Kiewel (via his parents), Gay Toltl Kinman, Jackie Lucio, Paul McKenzie, Dolly Secrist, Katherine Shephard, and Tom and Marie O'Day. Any similarities to the real person and the character portrayed are strictly coincidental.

I'd also like to thank Letty Olivas and Charlene Tess for their advice on procedures and character suggestions. Carole Aspinwall, thanks for proofreading. You did a great job. Lots and lots of kudos go to Dick Schwein, retired FBI Special Agent in Charge, who went beyond the call of duty. Harry Bronson is so much better because of you. Any errors in police procedure are strictly mine and not Dick's.

Another special thanks goes to author Bill Crider for all of his help, advice, and guidance. I'm deeply indebted to you, Bill. Same goes to all the fine folks at Five Star Mysteries, especially John Helfers.

There are moments in everyone's lives when we need to reach out and know someone's there to cheer us, cry with us, laugh with us, or give us moral support. That's where the Mystery Babes come in. Pat, thanks for suggesting my name for membership. You, Babes, mean the world to me. Thanks for everything. The Babes rock!

I'd also like to thank and send hugs to all of my readers.

Without you, I couldn't exist. I'd love to hear from you: lchayden@lycos.com. Feel free to visit my Web site www.lchayden.freeservers.com and sign my guest book.

A final, special, extra-warm thanks goes to my husband, Rich. My world without you wouldn't be a world at all—and Robert, my son, thanks for your suggestions with the geocaching. Thanks to all of my family for their support and love, especially the Bolds, Rich, Robert, Megan, Don, Lara, and Andrew.

Chapter 1

Sam slammed the newspaper down and threw the beer against the wall. It splattered like a splotchy starburst.

So Bronson was retiring. The famous Harry Bronson.

Dallas' finest.

He would now live a life of leisure and peace.

Not likely, not if Sam could help it. After all, Bronson had ruined Sam's life, and for that, Bronson would pay. Sam leaned back and thought of the plan that had been formulating for over a year. Now, finally, it could be executed.

Sam smiled.

Ever since his retirement, it had been Harry Bronson's job to retrieve the mail. No big thing, mailbox right at the edge of his property line. But the P.O. Box—that was a different story. Six blocks away and Bronson hated to drive. So he chose to walk, which he considered to be an excellent form of exercise. After all, Bronson was in his fifties, and he knew walking was good for him. But walking just to pick up the mail didn't entice him. What did appeal to him was its location. The building that stood next to the post office was a coffee shop—a Ma and Pa–type place where they knew how to make a good cup of coffee. Just thinking about the rich coffee bean smell caused Bronson to increase his pace.

That's one of the things Bronson missed most about retiring. Not too many places to get a good cup of coffee. His poor Carol—a real good woman, been married now thirty-four years—still couldn't make a good cup of coffee.

Sad, but true.

Bronson retrieved the key from his pocket, opened the mailbox and stared at it. Had someone sent one more envelope, the post office would have fined him for littering. He really should pick up his mail more often, or better yet, cancel this P.O. thing. Now that he no longer worked for the Dallas police department . . .

Bronson scooped all the mail, placed it in the bag he had specifically brought for this purpose, then hurried next door. He ordered a cup of Jamaican-me-crazy coffee, sat down at one of the tables, and emptied the bag.

Just as he had expected. Lots of junk mail, lots of bills. Nothing ever good.

Then he saw it. An envelope addressed to him similar to the one he had received a little over a week ago. Neither envelope had a return address. Its postmark, like the one before, told him it had also been sent from Dallas. Bronson opened the letter and read the typewritten text:

I didn't get an answer. Do you remember Casey?

S

Bronson clearly recalled the first typewritten message. It had read: *Remember Casey? S* had also signed it.

A stabbing pain, like thousands of needles penetrating his skin, immobilized Bronson.

Casey.

His first big case. His first failure.

Casey had died because Bronson had chosen to follow procedure.

Casey.

Dead now for over twenty years.

Twenty-odd years, and it still haunted him.

He had sworn back then that from there on, he'd follow his gut instinct even if it meant ignoring procedure. During the next twenty-six years that he spent on the force, he became infamous for bending the rules, just a little, now and then. Outside of his immediate supervisors, no one seemed to mind too much. After all, he almost always solved the cases.

Almost always.

But not Casey's.

Bronson's glance strayed toward the plain envelope, the type sold at thousands of discount stores, supermarkets, and drug or office supply stores. Tracing it would be next to impossible, but there existed more than one way to cook a goose. Or in this case, catch the goose.

Bronson drank his coffee, scooped the mail back into the bag, and hurried home. Once there, he dumped the mail on the couch, walked over to his desk and retrieved two swabs and a small plastic bottle filled with distilled water. He swabbed the sticky side of both of the envelope flaps and the stamps, placed the swabs in separate envelopes, labeled their contents, and sealed the envelopes.

Next, he made duplicates of both envelopes and their letters. He bagged the original letters and envelopes in separate plastic bags. He placed all of the items in a large envelope and labeled it *Paul McKenzie*.

First thing tomorrow, he would call him and cash in on a favor. Bronson would deliver the bag and Paul would use the swabs to do DNA testing, and from the original envelope, hopefully, he would lift some fingerprints that were on file. If nothing else, Paul could determine what kind of printer was used. The results would tell Bronson everything he needed to know. "Gotcha!" The goose was cooked and Bronson wondered why that was so important. He didn't even like goose.

Just as he stuffed everything inside the top drawer, the front door opened and Carol stepped in. "Whew!" She wiped her hands on the sides of her jeans. "I finished packing the camper. It's ready to go. Have you—" Her eyes narrowed as she studied her husband. She placed her hands on her hips. "Harry Bronson, are you brooding again about losing that job?"

Bronson frowned. "I was on the force over twenty-six years."

"Yeah, have you forgotten already? That's twenty-six looong years. So you just snap out of it. You promised me. One-month vacation time. No beeper. No cell phone. You are retired."

"Forced retirement, have you forgotten?"

Carol's eyes softened and Bronson realized why he loved this woman so much. He forced a smile. "Gotta take the cell phone, though. In case one of the kids needs to get hold of us." Amazing, he still thought of them as kids even though they were married and in their late twenties. He made a mental note to stop referring to them as kids.

"I'll give you that one. You can take the cell phone." Carol's eyes narrowed, studying her husband. "You're still brooding about being fired?"

Bronson shrugged and looked down.

She walked over to him and hugged him. "You know it was a political move. You and Garza never got along. He's strictly by the book. You weren't. You ruffled his feathers once too often. You knew it was coming. Only reason he didn't fire you sooner was because he knew how good you are. Hell, all of Dallas knows about you. You're a legend in this city."

"That doesn't change a thing, though." He massaged his temple. "I've been thinkin' about a P.I. license. Maybe I should get one of 'em. I'm too young to retire."

"You could do that, but first one month. Just you and me in our camper, touring the country. No work. You promised, remember?"

Yeah, but I hate to drive, but I did promise her, didn't I? He rearranged his features, hoping he had put on a happy face. "And a promise made is a debt unpaid." Bronson wrapped his arms around his wife and thought about the letter.

Certainly, it didn't mean anything. Just someone's way of letting him know that the great Harry Bronson wasn't infallible.

But Bronson already knew that.

He had botched Casey's case.

Somewhere out there in the streets, a killer walked. Free of guilt. Free of fear. He had challenged the police, and he had won.

All because Bronson followed procedure.

Chapter 2

Normally, Carol rose at the crack of dawn. But not today, a small miracle Bronson felt thankful for. He had told Carol not to worry about breakfast. "I'll be meetin' Paul for coffee and a doughnut." He knew she wouldn't question that. He had been, after all, a policeman.

His eyes snapped open even before the alarm clock went off. He quickly dressed as he listened to Carol gently snore. He quietly closed the bedroom door, and from his desk in the study, he retrieved the package containing the envelopes, letters, and swabs. He did all of this without arousing Carol's curiosity. Boy, he was good.

Fifteen minutes later, he pulled into the Dunkin' Donuts parking lot. Paul, a big man with a belly to match, sat at the corner booth table. He set the newspaper down and waved at Bronson. They made small talk until both had consumed their doughnuts. Paul wiped his mouth and looked at Bronson. "So what's up?"

"Meanin'?"

Paul pointed to the envelope. "Is that for me?"

Bronson gently slid it toward his side of the table. "As a matter of fact, yes. Darnest thing. Been gettin' these annoyin' letters. Thought maybe you could unofficially check them out for me. See what kind of information you can find."

"DNA? Fingerprints?"

Bronson nodded. "The works."

"And I bet you want me to do this on the sly?"

"Preferably." He looked down at the receipt. "I'll even pay for your coffee and doughnut."

Paul gave him a quizzical look. "We've already paid. We went Dutch." His eyes sparkled with laughter.

"Next time, then." Bronson pushed the envelope a few inches toward Paul.

Paul reached for the envelope. "Sure. I've got nothing to do anyway."

Bronson smiled. He knew Paul had enough work to keep twenty men employed.

Back home, Bronson glared at the budget figures. Maybe if he did that long enough, they'd magically transform themselves into numbers that would make ends meet at the end of the month. He glared some more, but nothing changed.

Now would be the time to cuss, but Carol would shoot him if he did. And that wouldn't be good. He still had a lot of things he wanted to accomplish.

To be honest, he loved his new RV. Small, only twenty-five feet long, but with the two slide-outs, Bronson felt no desire for a larger one. This unit contained all the luxuries of home. The nice-size bed on the back didn't have to be converted every night from a sofa or dinette. The bathroom contained a shower with a small tub. The living area had a TV, microwave, an oven, a good-size refrigerator complete with a freezer, and plenty of storage space. Who could ask for more?

While Bronson loved the RV, he hated the hefty payment that went along with it. Add to that the tow vehicle. His old Ford hadn't been made to be towed. Something about transmissions. Only certain cars were made to be towed flat.

So now, Bronson had become the proud owner of a green Honda CRV. Cute thing, sure enough, but it also had a cute monthly bill attached to it. Guys at work all knew this, so they contributed to Bronson's retirement fund. They raised—bless their souls—a bit over three thousand dollars. Surely, a nice sum, but eventually, the money would run out. Then the camper would sit in their driveway, unused. Too expensive to move. So why have it?

This retirement thing—Bronson just wasn't ready for it. But he had promised Carol at least a month-long vacation, and heaven knew she deserved it.

The phone rang and out of instinct, Bronson glanced at the caller I.D. Briefly, he wondered if it was work, then remembered. No, of course, it wouldn't be. He picked up the receiver. "Yeah?" and immediately regretted it. It sounded more like a snap than a greeting. "I mean, hello?"

A brief pause followed then, "Is this Bronson? Detective Harry Bronson?"

"You could say that."

"This is Wayne Weeks, Events Coordinator at the Sun Lodge in Safford. I—"

"Where?"

"Safford."

Never heard of it. Bronson retrieved a notepad and wrote down Wayne Weeks—Events Coordinator: Sun Lodge—Safford.

Weeks, as though reading Bronson's mind said, "That's Safford, Arizona."

"Uh-huh."

"Ever heard of a group called The Slayers?"

Bronson searched his memory bank. Nothing clicked. "Nope, can't say I have. Sorry. Are they some music group?"

"Hardly." Weeks' tone hardened, as though he'd been put out. "Allow me—"

"Look here." Bronson glanced down at the notepad. "Weeks, is it? What exactly is it that you're sellin'?"

"I'm not selling. I'm looking to hire you."

Now the man was talking. "I'm no longer with the police department."

"I know."

"I'm not a private detective, either."

"I know."

"I'm just a citizen."

"I know."

This Weeks person knew a lot. That bothered Bronson. "I'm listenin'."

"Back to The Slayers."

Bronson wrote down the name. "Go on."

"Ever heard of Dorothy L. Sayers?"

Now that name, Bronson knew. "My wife—she's a reader. Favorites are mysteries. Seems she's read some of Sayers' work. She was a British mystery author from the 1940s or '50s. Are you talkin' about the same person?"

"The one and only."

"Uh-huh." Bronson wrote down Dorothy L. Sayers—mystery author.

"That leads me to The Slayers. It's a rather large group of—now, how should I phrase this?—aficionados of the mystery genre. Most members live in the Phoenix or Tucson areas, but they come from all over Arizona. You can see how they chose their name. It's to honor Dorothy L. Sayers, but since they're a mystery group, they're the Slayers, instead of Sayers."

Cute, but what does that have to do with me, Bronson thought as he skimmed through his notes. Nothing there to give him a clue. "So how does this lead to a job?"

"Once a year, The Slayers put on a—what should I call

17

it?—a week-long convention? Monday is the day everyone arrives. Not much going on, just mainly socializing. Tuesday, the ground rules are laid out."

Rules? "What kind of rules?" Bronson, who had been writing everything down furiously, used the temporary pause to wiggle his fingers.

"There's going to be a murder, Detective Bronson, not a real one, of course. It's just something the group makes up. They break into teams and they have the next three days to solve the crime. Friday night all of the losing teams treat the winners to a nice meal at our local steak house, Brick's. After dinner, the winners are given the trophy that they get to keep until the next, uh, convention. Saturday, the group spends celebrating and comparing notes. Sunday, after their usual good-bye breakfast, everyone packs the suitcases and leaves."

"Sounds like these people are playin' a game."

"It is that, but it's a harmless game, and each year they contribute to Safford's economy, so we always welcome them."

"So what we're talkin' about here is one of those dinner/murder theater things."

"I suppose you could say that, except that it's a week-long convention."

"Fascinatin', but where do I come in?"

"The Slayers have a consultant, someone the contestants can turn to. It's up to the consultant how much he wants to tell them, and what questions he wants to answer. But he's always available, twenty-four hours a day for those three days." Weeks paused and cleared his throat. "Unfortunately, their consultant for the past seven years was involved in a—what shall I call it?—a serious car accident and won't be doing that anymore. Would you be interested in the position?"

Yeah, sure. He would be a great one to tell them about proper procedure. "Give me some specifics."

"Pay is excellent, considering you're working only a few days. Before you leave, you'll receive a check for a thousand dollars, and on top of that, all of your fees to the convention are paid. That includes the admission fee, all of your meals, and the motel room."

"I have a camper."

"Roper Lake has some very fine facilities. We'll pay that, too, or you can park your camper in the motel's parking lot. There's plenty of room. Your choice." He paused as though giving Bronson an opportunity to digest his words. "I've got a brochure that will answer all your questions and then some more. I can drop it in the mail today, if you're interested, and you should have it by tomorrow. Or if you have a fax . . ."

"No, no fax." That was another thing Bronson missed about work. He put down his pen and tapped the notepad. "I have one question which I know won't be answered in the brochure. How did you get my name?"

"I read the article in the Dallas newspaper about you retiring. It mentioned that you've got a motor home and plan to do some traveling. I've got a camper myself, and I'm always looking for places to spend the night for free. I bet you will be, too. So, do I send you the information?"

It wouldn't hurt to take a look. Besides, something in Bronson's gut told him there was more to this than just a game. "Give me five minutes. I need to talk it over with the missus."

"Of course, I'll call back in five minutes."

"You do that." Bronson hung up and retrieved the caller I.D. number. Area code 928. He took out the map that listed the area codes and looked up Arizona. The area code matched for the Safford area. Next, Bronson looked up the

Sun Lodge on the Internet. The number on his caller I.D. and the one listed on the Internet were the same. He dialed the number.

"Is this the motel where Wayne Weeks works?"

"Yes, sir, he's our Events Coordinator. Would you like for me to connect you to him?"

"Not right now. I just wanted to make sure I had the right coordinator attached to the right motel."

"You do."

"Good. Thank you." Bronson hung up and stared at his notes.

If he did that long enough, something would surely jump out.

It always did.

This time it didn't.

The phone rang. The caller I.D. identified the caller as Weeks. Five minutes sure went fast. Bronson gave him the address and added, "There's one more question."

"Go ahead."

"You said you read the article about me in the Dallas paper."

"That's right."

"What's a Dallas paper doin' in Safford?"

A small pause followed. "You know, I can't really remember. But the paper was lying around somewhere, and I happened to see the article."

"That's unusual."

"No, not really. This is a motel. People are forever bringing newspapers from different cities. They read the paper and leave it here."

Bronson supposed that made sense, but he still made a note of it. He thanked Weeks and hung up. He continued to stare at his notes.

One word jumped out.

Safford.

That's where he would go.

Safford, the city that began with an *S*.

Chapter 3

"You've been pounding at that computer now for hours. What exactly is it you're looking for?"

Bronson turned to face his wife. He removed his glasses and set them down.

Carol took a step forward. "My god, Harry Bronson. You've gone and accepted a job. Haven't you?"

Now how did she know that? Maybe she should join the police department. "Not exactly." He walked toward her.

"What does 'not exactly' mean? You either did or you didn't."

Bronson led her to the couch. "Sit down. We need to talk."

"I think I'm not going to like what you have to say, Harry Bronson."

"And I think I don't like it when you call me by my full name. Reminds me of Mom. She used my full name when I did somethin' wrong."

"So did you do something wrong, Harry . . . Bronson?"

Dang that woman. If she didn't make him feel like a naughty child. "Ever heard of Safford?"

Carol shook her head.

"It's a city in Arizona, about two hours away from Tucson. They have a lake just on the outskirts of town. That'll be Roper Lake. It's got real nice campin' facilities, and you can swim in the lake or fish. Part of Roper Lake is Dankworth

Ponds for fishin'. And it's got a nice walkin' trail. Some more trails at Roper Lake. I got pictures on the Internet that I can show you. Looks nice. Real nice. Very relaxing. Beautiful scenery. Right dab in the middle of the desert, but it's got plenty of trees."

Carol stared at Bronson through eyes that seemed both bottomless and captivating, like a student paying close attention to the teacher. "So far, so good. Keep talking."

"Close by is Kartchner Caverns State Park. That's that new cave they just opened a couple of years ago. It's the big rave of the Southwest. Arizona is using the latest technology to keep the cave alive. That in itself is worth the trip."

Carol leaned back and stared at the far-off corner. Bronson wondered if she could see the caverns from there. Or worse, maybe she was staring at the hole on the wall he had promised to fix five years ago. After a slight pause, she said, "Sounds even better."

Good, she hadn't mentioned the hole. "There's more. Mt. Graham and that Discover thing—they're there, too, and—"

"Stop with the Chamber of Commerce information. I want to hear about the job part."

"Oh." Bronson explained about the game and how he would serve as a consultant. "So you see, it's not a real job. I'm just there to play this game, and they pay all expenses. And we can use the thousand dollars to expand the trip. We can stay in the area a bit longer. I'd take you to the cave, and Mt. Graham, and—"

"Yes."

"Did I tell you about the hot springs? They're—" Surely, Bronson hadn't heard what he thought he heard. "What did you say?"

"I said, 'Yes'."

Well, hot-diggity-dog. And here he thought he'd have

trouble convincing her. "I called the Safford Chamber of Commerce. They're sendin' us a bunch of information. They're real nice folks. You'll like it in Safford."

"I already said yes." Carol walked up to Bronson and kissed his lips. "You can stop with the P.R. work." She pointed to the hole on the wall. "It's still there, you know."

Dang, she had noticed it. "Right after supper, I'll fix it."

"You do that. In the meantime, while you're waiting for supper, finish up whatever you were doing. Supper will be ready in about ten minutes."

"Actually, all I have is one more thing to look up." He went back to the computer and typed the search engine's name. When the page popped up, he clicked on the white pages, keying in Safford, Arizona.

He scrolled down to the S's and read the residents' names. Just as he had suspected, he found it. The tip of his finger stroked the name.

Dolly Secrist.

His connection to Safford.

Dolly, Casey's mother.

Bronson looked away from the monitor and wondered if it really would be wise to drag Carol to Safford.

Chapter 4

The next week flew by like a tornado touching ground here and there. A zillion things needed to be done: find a house sitter, arrange for the mail, mow the lawn, pay bills, cancel the paper, even clean the house. Why in heaven's name clean the house?

It seemed to Bronson that if they were leaving for a month or more, cleaning the house used up energy better used elsewhere. Surely, dirt would invade the house while they were gone. So why clean? Wasted energy, he had told Carol, but she insisted, so they cleaned.

Then there was the packing. Was Carol really serious? Did she really need to take all those items? Goodness, they were going to be gone for a month, not a year—unless Carol had plans that she hadn't revealed. Bronson bit his lip. Nah, she wouldn't do that.

And speaking of packing, there was one thing he should pack, and he might as well do it now while Carol was busy cleaning the upstairs. He went to his study, removed the picture, opened the safe, and stared at his gun collection. He had hoped that once he retired, he wouldn't have to use a gun, but better safe than sorry.

He reached for the five-shot, snub-nosed revolver and a box of ammunition, closed the safe, replaced the picture, and headed for the car. He opened the trunk and hid his cache under the spare tire.

Now he had packed.

He rushed back inside and continued working on the list of One Thousand Things That Needed to Be Done before they could leave. *One thing for sure, this going on a nice, relaxed vacation sure puts the stress in my life. I'd rather be workin'.*

But now, as they headed west on Interstate 40, Bronson could see that excitement enveloped Carol. She looked forward to this vacation and her excitement filled him with a sense of wonderment. Maybe it wouldn't be so bad, this traveling.

Bronson was even beginning to push this Casey *S* thing to the back of his mind. He hadn't even gotten around to calling Paul and following up on the fingerprint and DNA results. Not that that mattered. Had Paul found something, he would have called.

One thing that pleased Bronson was that he hadn't heard from *S*. That probably meant that it had been someone's idea of a sick joke. But now it was over or at least he hoped so.

After all, they hadn't yet reached Safford where he planned to contact Casey's mother, Dolly Secrist. If she had sent those notes, then he had nothing to worry about. Dolly was as gentle as a lamb.

Carol's voice interrupted Bronson's thoughts.

"Look at the size of that cross." Carol moved her index finger to her right.

She didn't need to point. No way Bronson could have missed the gigantic cross. It had to be close to two hundred feet tall. "Want to take a closer look?"

Carol nodded and Bronson pulled off the highway and followed the access road to the parking lot. Once there, he scanned the area. He saw a red truck, pulling a white trailer. He also spotted a Class C motor home and three sedans (blue, black, and red). Two of the cars had Texas tags. The other one was from Missouri.

An elderly couple, holding hands, headed toward the motor home. Other people stood by the life-size bronze statues arranged in a wide circle. Each statue depicted the various stages of the cross, beginning with Jesus' capture and ending with His empty tomb. Toward the back, on a hill, steps led to a resurrected Jesus. Bronson took all of this in, but mainly he concentrated on the people.

"Harry Bronson!"

Startled, Bronson turned to Carol. "What did I do now?"

"You're working."

"Workin'? How can you say I'm workin'? I'm in . . . in . . . where am I?"

"We're close to Groom, Texas."

"Ah, yes. Good ol' Groom, Texas. I'm in Groom, Texas, starin' at the biggest cross I've ever seen, and you say I'm workin'?"

"You were studying people."

Bronson shrugged. "Old habits die hard." He reached for Carol's hand and led her toward the cross. They stopped to admire the first bronze sculpture that depicted the journey of Jesus Christ to Calvary, then moved on to the second one.

That's when Bronson first noticed it. It came like a prickle in the back of his neck. He had felt the same thing many times at work, and he knew exactly what it meant.

Someone was watching him.

He stood alert, like a bird ready to take flight. His gaze darted from sculpture to sculpture. He saw a young couple, standing close together. The young man had his arm wrapped around his gal. A middle-aged woman with a bright, colorful blouse shielded her eyes as she stared at the top of the cross. Two elderly men, both wearing green shirts, headed toward a small building on the west side of the property. A family huddled together at the foot of a statue of a resurrected Jesus.

These people were tourists. No one paid any attention to him.

Still . . .

Bronson shook himself, forcing his feelings aside.

As Carol looked at the Tomb for the Unborn, Bronson once again grasped the opportunity to glance around. No new faces. No surprises.

Carol turned to stare at him.

Bronson smiled.

She smiled back.

He led her to the small building and they stepped in.

Carol gasped. "Look! It's a replica of the Shroud of Turin." She squeezed her husband's hand.

Bronson nodded.

"Do you think they'll let me take a picture?"

Bronson shrugged. "Dunno. I don't see any signs saying No Photographs, but ask her." He pointed to a young lady who answered the questions the two men in green asked. Carol headed toward the clerk.

Bronson stepped outside. Another family had arrived and a woman, apparently by herself, moved from statue to statue.

He felt someone touch his arm. He turned and faced Carol.

"Did you see it?" she asked him.

"Who?"

"Not who. What. Did you see the Shroud of Turin?"

"Of course. It's so . . . big."

"Big?" Carol frowned. "Okay. Out with it."

"Out with what?"

"You can't fool me, Harry Bronson. Something's going on, and I want to be in on it."

Dang that woman, but when she's right, she's right. Something was going on, but Bronson couldn't quite place it.

"I was thinkin'. This is our first tourist stop after I retired. We should sign the guest book. Think they'll have one there?" He pointed to an even smaller building that presumably housed the gift shop. Maybe whoever was watching him had sneaked in there.

"Harry Bronson!"

Bronson grabbed her hand and pulled her along. "Come on, let's go sign in." While Carol signed the guest book and browsed around the small shop, Bronson stepped back and watched other people.

No one looked him directly in the eye, but also, no one avoided him. Maybe Carol was right. His being in a working mode had caused him to think someone lurked behind the bush, or in this case, behind the statue.

Carol glanced through the postcard selections, and Bronson helped her select two. With her purchases in hand, she read aloud the information on the postcard as they walked back to the camper. "Says here this cross is visible up to twenty miles. It contains seventy-five tons of steel and . . ."

Bronson stopped listening.

He noticed a piece of paper stuck to his windshield. None of the other cars in the parking lot had notes. He grabbed it and quickly opened the door for Carol.

He walked around to the driver's side of the camper and looked down at the paper. He stuffed it in his pants pocket and climbed into the driver's compartment.

"What's with the paper?"

"Nothin'. Just a pledge card, askin' for donations for this place." He started the engine and carefully pulled away.

His thoughts turned to the card he had stuffed in his pocket. On it, using large block letters, someone had written, "CASEY WOULD HAVE LIKED THIS PLACE." It was signed *S*.

Chapter 5

Bronson eyed the sign that read *Amarillo eighteen miles*. "We can eat in the camper or we could stop at a restaurant. Amarillo is about twenty minutes from here."

Carol looked at her watch. "It's a bit early for dinner, but I guess we could stop at a fast-food place. I'm not in the mood for a large supper, and I'd really rather not cook while we're rolling."

Bronson spotted a McDonald's sign. "Mickey D's okay with you?"

"Sure, why not?"

Bronson pulled into the McDonald's parking lot. They got out and ordered their food.

"I forgot my cell," Bronson said. "I'm going back to the camper. You wait here and get our food. I'll join you in a minute."

He hurried toward the camper, his shoes echoing his urgency.

Once inside, he retrieved the note from his pocket and placed it in a plastic bag. He stuffed it in an envelope, addressed it to Paul McKenzie, sealed the envelope, put on a stamp, and placed it back in his pocket. He would mail it tonight from the campground.

He locked the door behind him and rushed back to McDonald's. Halfway there, he stopped and headed back to the camper. He had forgotten to get the cell.

Soon as they sat down to eat, Carol opened the atlas. "I definitely want to stop in Albuquerque. There's a place called Old Town where we could . . ."

Bronson bit into his hamburger and washed it down with coffee. McDonald's coffee, not the best, but not bad at all. At least he was glad to be drinking coffee. What he wasn't glad about was that he hadn't taken the time to call Paul. He had assumed the letters had been a sick practical joke, and that nothing else would happen.

He had assumed—something a veteran cop should never do. He knew better. First chance he had, he'd contact Paul.

They finished eating and as they headed back to the camper, Carol was still discussing Albuquerque.

"Shiiit!" Bronson said.

Carol stopped and grabbed her husband's arm. "What?" Her gaze bounced from object to object.

"We have a flat."

Carol looked at the camper.

"The car," Bronson said.

Carol saw it and nodded. "We have a spare, don't we?"

That, they did. "Yeah," Bronson grumbled. He hated to fix flats. "You go inside the camper and read your book while I fix this thing."

"You sure, now? Nothing I can do to help?"

"Fixin' a flat is a one-person job. You go on, make yourself comfortable in the camper."

Carol's lips brushed Bronson's cheek. "Thank you, honey." She turned and headed for the camper while Bronson retrieved from the trunk all the items he would need.

He sat in front of the tire and looked at it.

Someone had slashed it.

Bronson looked all around, but he couldn't tell if *S* was watching him.

★ ★ ★ ★ ★

As soon as they settled in the campground, Bronson said, "Why don't you take your shower first? I think I'll go outside and enjoy the cool evenin' breeze."

"Sounds like a plan," Carol said and headed to the bedroom.

Bronson waited until he heard the water running before he stepped out of the camper and headed for the public phone booth. From memory, he dialed Paul McKenzie's home phone number.

The phone rang and rang.

Bronson gently hung up. His thoughts strayed from the message on the pledge card to the slashed tire. Someone was definitely playing some game with him. He wished he'd been able to talk to Paul. He headed for the office, mailed the envelope, and returned to the phone booth. Knowing Paul, he was probably still at work. Bronson deposited the mandatory coins and dialed Paul's work number.

Paul picked up on the second ring. "Lab. McKenzie speaking."

"Hey, Paul. How's it goin'?"

"Not so good, buddy. I have nothing useful. From the envelope we lifted a couple of fingerprints. Yours and several unknowns. I ran them through AFIS. No match. I tried the letter. I thought maybe I could match one of those prints with the ones from the letter."

"And?"

"And the letter didn't have any prints. Not a one."

"The stamp?"

"No prints there."

"DNA?"

"There was a trace of DNA but nothing to compare it to."

"And the type on the letter and envelope?"

"Comes from a common printer sold at all Wal-Marts and K-Marts nationwide. Office Depot and Office Max carries them. So does Best Buy, Circuit City, Staples. Independent computer stores sell them. Then there's the used market and we haven't even mentioned the Internet."

Damn.

"Someone went to a lot of trouble to make sure you didn't find out who sent you that letter."

"I noticed." And it had to be someone familiar with police procedure. Maybe one of the guys at work had sent it after all, but that didn't explain the note on the windshield, and certainly no one from work would ever slash a tire. But he'd check, just in case. "You know anybody in my old unit takin' vacation time around now?"

"Not a one."

"Personal time off?"

"Bronson, you're thinking it's someone from here?"

"Not too many choices there. Had to be someone who was familiar with the case."

"Bronson, you know us. We like to play jokes on each other, but nothing like this. Never."

"I've received another note."

A slight pause followed, then, "Damn. Where? When?"

"This mornin'. Someone left it on my windshield at a tourist stop."

"Oh, God. That means he's following you."

"You've got that right."

"Should make it easier to track. Soon you'll see the same car, the same person showing up wherever you go."

"Thought so, too. Thing is, we're at a campground. Only saw one camper at the parkin' lot this mornin'. Driven by an elderly couple. They're not staying here. I checked. As I drove in, I scoped the campground. Not one car, not one camper was familiar. I plan to walk the area as soon as I finish talkin' to you, but I doubt I'll find a familiar car or camper."

"And the note?"

"It's on the way to you, but I doubt you'll find anythin' useful."

"It's worth a try."

"Yep, it is." Bronson momentarily paused. "Son of a bitch also slashed my tire."

"Are you and Carol all right?"

"Oh yeah. At least he had the decency to do it while Carol and I were eatin' at McDonald's."

"At least that's something."

They chatted for a bit longer, then Bronson hung up.

On his way back to his motor home, he took the long way around and studied each camper and its tow vehicle.

He found nothing new, but he hadn't expected to find anything. Yet someone was following him. How was that possible? He headed back to his camper, but instead of going in, he slowly walked around the camper. Then he got on all fours and looked under the camper. Nothing there.

The car, then. That would make more sense. He walked around it and once again got on all fours. It didn't take him long to find the tracking device. He looked around. No one seemed to be paying any attention to him. He placed the transmitter on the car next to him. He hoped they were heading in the opposite direction.

Across from the campground, Sam sat in the car. A pair of binoculars lay on the passenger seat.

Sam smiled. One thing about Bronson, he always had a unique sense of humor.

But in spite of that, Bronson looked agitated. He hadn't used his cell phone to make his call. Chances were he didn't want the little missus to find out what was going on. He wouldn't want her to feel threatened. He had to make sure she was safe. Not by a long shot, Sam thought.

"Game's over," Sam said to the driver. "Bronson found the tracking device. I knew he would eventually. I was just hoping he wouldn't find it so soon. No matter. Let's head for Safford. We'll wait for him there."

Chapter 6

Ah, Albuquerque. A most delightful town, especially here in the older section. Quaint little stores lined the streets of Old Town. Too many shopping temptations for my Carol, Bronson thought. He wrapped his hand around hers, partly to hold her, but also to keep her from running inside each store.

Carol stopped, looked at a window display, dropped her husband's hand, and dashed inside the store. He found a little coffee shop and waited for Carol to rejoin him. Half an hour later, she came out carrying a small bag. That was good. Couldn't have spent too much. Then he remembered that diamonds come in very small packages. Better not to ask. Sometimes ignorance was bliss.

"The cashier told me about the National History Museum. It sounds very interesting." Carol looked at her husband and smiled with her eyes.

When she did that, Bronson couldn't resist her. He'd tame a dinosaur, if she asked him to. Bronson got instructions to the museum and drove them there.

Once they reached the museum, Carol delighted in the historical displays. Bronson felt more compelled to study the visitors. Two, he noticed, were the same middle-aged couple he had seen this morning at Old Town. Bronson watched them until they walked out of the museum, fifteen minutes later.

Bronson kissed Carol on the cheek. "I'm goin' to find the Little Boys' Room. See you in a while." Bronson walked past the restroom and out the main door. He watched as the couple approached their car, a '56 Chevy. Unless this couple drove two cars, the vintage Chevy had not been one of the cars parked at the large cross parking lot in Groom, Texas, or in the campground.

Bronson made a mental note and rejoined Carol.

At exactly two in the morning, Bronson's cell rang. His eyes snapped open. Emergency at work? Or, worse, one of the kids? Where was he? Certainly not at home. Where, then?

Oh, yeah, the camper parked at a campground in Socorro.

He no longer worked.

The kids!

In two long strides he reached the phone. "Hello?"

Silence.

Bronson sucked in his breath. "Who's this?"

The answer came in the form of a whisper. "Casey."

Bronson felt the impact of the word like a punch to his stomach. He kept the telephone glued to his ear even though he knew the connection had been broken.

S has my cell number. How's this possible? Bronson looked at his cell phone. He was in an analog zone, not a digital zone. That meant his caller I.D. would not register the call. Had *S* known that?

Bronson called customer service. "I've just received a call, but my caller I.D. didn't pick it up. Can you please give me that number?"

The employee explained that would be impossible. "I'm really sorry, but there's no way we can get that number for you."

Bronson thanked him and hung up.

"What was that about?" Carol sat up in bed, her open hands rested on her upper chest, like the heroine of a silent movie.

"I thought you were in the habit of ignorin' calls in the middle of the night."

"I was when you were working. Was that one of the kids?"

"No. It was . . . an obscene caller. I tried to get his number from the company, but the guy I talked to said that was impossible. Wonder if I could have gotten it if I were still a detective?"

"You sure that's all it was—just an obscene call?"

"Believe me. It was obscene." Bronson walked over to Carol and kissed her forehead. "Go back to sleep. Sorry the call woke you up."

Carol smiled, lay back down, and covered herself. Within minutes, Bronson heard her snore gently. He lay beside her and made sure he didn't move so he wouldn't wake her. As he listened to his wife's gentle breathing pattern, Bronson wished luck would visit him. He tried to force himself to sleep, but instead, he remained wide awake, staring at the darkness that swallowed him.

Chapter 7

Bronson sat in his motor home parked across the street from the Sun Lodge. His unblinking eyes stared at the Lodge. In all of his years working as a detective, he had never once stayed in such a luxurious place. It was always the smallest, least expensive places that he registered for. This, on the other hand, well, what could he say? Except maybe this retirement life, he could get used to it.

He smiled and realized Carol had been talking to him. "Huh?"

"I said, why are we just sitting here?"

"I was . . . just checking the parking lot. Remember, I don't like to drive, especially a big monster like this, but I've got to admit: I'm gettin' used to it, and I'm almost likin' it." He checked out the parking lot. "Reckon I could park over there, on the side."

"You do that. I can't wait to see the inside and then relax."

"Be careful now. I don't want you too relaxed." Bronson wiggled his eyebrows.

"In that case, let's hurry up and get in there." Carol pointed to the motel and wiggled her eyebrows.

Bronson looked at his wife and flashed her his bone-melting grin.

An hour and a half later, Bronson and Carol lay in bed, a broad smile plastered on Bronson's face. Carol snuggled in closer to her husband. "I know you've got work to do, so let me tell you my plans. First, I'm going to do a couple of laps in the indoor pool, hit the exercise room, then take the longest shower in history. Afterwards, I'm going to read the new Bill Crider mystery."

"That sounds nice." Bronson kissed Carol, got up, and headed for the bathroom. "Unfortunately, I'm a workin' man and have no time for such luxuries. I'm goin' to take a look around."

"Don't expect me to feel sorry for you. You'll enjoy every minute of it."

Probably would, if S wasn't around. "You know me too well." He threw her a kiss and stepped into the shower.

Twenty minutes later, he headed toward the lobby, stopped at the registration desk, and asked directions.

The woman behind the counter at the motel's lobby told Bronson that Staghorn Avenue intercepted U.S. Highway 191.

"Lookin' at a time frame, what does that mean?"

The receptionist shrugged and smiled. "Maybe ten minutes at the most."

Bronson nodded. "Reckon everythin' over here is ten minutes away."

Without smiling the receptionist looked at Bronson. "Not necessarily. Some places are fifteen minutes away."

Bronson extended his index finger and moved it as though saluting her. "Gotcha," he said and walked out.

Bronson didn't reach Dolly Secrist's house in ten minutes. It took him a full thirteen minutes, Bronson noted. As he turned down Staghorn Avenue, Bronson recalled that it had been over twenty years since he had last seen Dolly.

Shortly after Casey's death, Bronson had kept in touch

with Dolly, but gradually the days turned into months and the months into years. Except for an occasional Christmas card, Bronson had not heard from Dolly. He wondered if she would even recognize him.

Here goes nothin'. He rang the doorbell and while he waited, he tried to calculate Dolly's age. Probably in her early seventies, he reasoned.

The door swung opened. A petite woman, barely five feet tall with short, stylish, white hair, looked up at Bronson. Her eyes squinted as she focused on him.

Bronson smiled. "Hello, Dolly, ma'am. I'm—"

"Harry Bronson." She smiled.

"Yes, ma'am. That would be me."

Dolly threw the screen door open and hugged Bronson. For a second, Bronson imagined his mom doing the same thing. He hadn't thought of his mother in ages. A pang of loneliness hit Bronson.

"Come in, come in. It's so good to see you."

Bronson stepped inside and closed the front door behind him. The living room wasn't anything like he expected. Instead of an orderly home, Bronson saw bright throw pillows and toys scattered throughout the room. An unfinished crossword puzzle and a pencil rested on the couch.

Bronson's gaze traveled from one framed picture to the other. Portraits of Dolly's children with their families adorned the walls. An eight-by-ten color print of Casey—the same one Bronson carried in his wallet—rested on the mantel. On the coffee table sat a picture of Dolly as a child, wearing her ballerina outfit.

Dolly pointed to the pastel flower-design sofa. "Sit." She closed the book that was on the reclining chair. "I was just reading a book on angels." She pointed to the book. "Have you read it yet?"

Bronson looked at the book. "No, ma'am. Can't say I have."

"You ought to try it. You'll like it." She folded her hands neatly in her lap. "Tell me, do you still like coffee like you used to?"

The possibility of drinking a good cup of coffee brought a smile to Bronson's face. He moved some Tinker toys and a child's book, *The Giving Tree*, aside and sat down. "To be truthful, ma'am, I've been havin' coffee withdrawals. I've been travelin' with my Carol, and she's a great little lady, but she knows nothin' about makin' a good cup of coffee. I could surely use one if it's not too much trouble."

"None at all." Dolly sprang to her feet and headed for the kitchen.

Bronson followed her to the big, country-style kitchen with wide-open spaces. An old-fashioned oval oak table and four upholstered chairs in front of a large bay window over-looked the backyard.

"Excuse the mess." Dolly pointed to the scattered toys. "For the past month, I've been babysitting my grandson while my daughter's at work."

Bronson nodded.

"Sammy Ryan Kiewel."

"Huh?"

"That's my grandson. Sammy. He's four."

The discarded Matchbox cars reminded Bronson of his own fascination with toy cars as a little kid. He looked up and found Dolly studying him.

Immediately, she broke eye contact. "He hardly takes a nap anymore, but today I got him to sleep."

"Ah." The aroma of coffee brewing tickled his nostrils.

"So what brings you to Safford? It's a long drive from Dallas."

"That it is." He reached for the cup of coffee Dolly handed him. He poured some milk and took three spoons of sugar. Good thing Carol wasn't around to see that. "I'm retired now, you know."

Dolly touched her nose. "No, I didn't know that. I would have never guessed that you would retire."

Bronson looked at her and noticed that she tapped her foot as she looked away. *What aren't you telling me?* Aloud, he said, "I reckon part of me will always be workin'." He sipped his coffee. "Ah, good coffee. Real good." He set the cup down. "I'm here for that mystery convention."

"Oh, really? I read in the newspaper about Safford hosting that conference. I never would have figured you to be one of the players."

"I'm not a player. I'm goin' to be their consultant." He sipped his coffee. "But then I thought you already knew that."

"What would make you think I'd know that?" She focused her attention on her fingernails.

"You get the *Dallas Mornin' News*?"

Dolly nodded. "I never cancelled my subscription after I left Dallas."

"Did you happen to see the small article about me retirin'? Thought maybe you read it and suggested my name to Wayne Weeks."

Dolly's lips formed what could be considered a weak smile. "Why, yes. I saw the article about you in the paper. But I didn't—" She rubbed her eyelid and looked away. "Did you say Wayne Weeks? He's the one who hired you?"

"Yes, ma'am."

"I know Wayne."

"Thought you would."

"That doesn't mean I gave him your name."

"But you could have."

"But I didn't give it to him." Dolly crossed her arms and stared at Bronson. "Talk to me, Bronson. What's going on? Why are you really here?"

"I told you. I've been hired . . ." Bronson spotted the teddy bear–shaped cookie jar. He opened it. "Chocolate chip cookies!"

"Homemade."

"Yeah? They go real good with coffee, but my cup happens to be empty."

Dolly reached for Bronson's cup. "I'll refill it, and you help yourself to some cookies. But leave some for Sammy. They're his favorites, and he'll expect some when he wakes up."

"That means I'll have to fight the little one for the cookies."

"If you do, you better be careful. Sammy takes his cookies very seriously."

"Ah, just my luck."

Dolly refilled the cup and handed it to Bronson.

He accepted it, took the milk out of the refrigerator, poured some into his coffee, and returned the milk to the refrigerator. He scooped three spoonfuls of sugar.

"All that sugar isn't good for you."

"That's what my Carol tells me, but I have cut back to three. Maybe soon I'll cut back some more. Maybe do two and a half, or a bit more." He looked up and smiled.

"You never answered me." She folded her arms.

Bronson smiled again.

Dolly shook her head. "You can be the most frustrating person in the world."

"Is that so?" He drank his coffee.

Dolly waited for Bronson to say something. When he didn't, she frowned and sighed. "Is this about . . . Casey?"

"You tell me, ma'am. Is it?" He bit into his cookie.

Dolly looked away. She walked over to the breakfast nook and sat down. She closed the Robert Parker novel she was reading.

Bronson joined her. "That's another book you're reading?"

Dolly nodded.

"Thought you were reading the one about angels."

"I am, but I'm also reading this one. I usually read three or four books at a time."

"Uh-huh." Bronson sipped his coffee. "You knew Weeks had hired me."

Dolly's nod was barely perceptible. "He told you?"

"Haven't talked to him."

"Then how did you know?"

"The look on your face when I knocked on your door. You weren't surprised to see me. It was more like you were expectin' me." Bronson blew into his cup and swallowed some coffee. "So here I am."

A long silence stretched between the two. Bronson watched as Dolly's lips began to quiver. "Wayne told me you're . . . you're . . . retired. How could you? What about Casey? Will her killer go forever unpunished?"

"Well, ma'am, let me put it this way. When I walked out of the office, I made a copy of each paper in one particular file. I'll let you guess which file that was."

"Casey's."

Bronson nodded and finished his coffee.

"I want cookies, too."

Bronson turned toward the source of the voice.

Sammy stood with his hands resting on his hips and a determined look stamped on his face.

Bronson opened the cookie jar and looked inside. "Look

here. There's some chocolate chip cookies in there, and they've got your name on 'em."

Sammy's eyes opened so wide they reminded Bronson of two saucers. "What's my name?"

"Well, let me look again." Bronson made a big production of staring inside the cookie jar. "I reckon they say Sammy Ryan Kiewel."

Sammy gasped. "That's me!"

"Then get over here and grab some—if it's okay with Grandma."

Dolly nodded and opened her arms. "But first, come here. Give Grandma a big kiss."

Sammy ran toward her and threw his arms around her neck. "I forgive you, Grandma, for making me go to sleep."

"Thank God!" Dolly smiled and the love she felt oozed out of her. She walked over to the refrigerator, retrieved the milk, and poured Sammy a glass. She set it on the table, next to the cookies.

Bronson stood up. "Best I be goin'." He gently punched Sammy on the arm. "You take real good care of Grandma."

"I do." Sammy bit his cookie. "She's my responsibility."

Bronson laughed. "That's a big word for a little fellow like you."

"I'm four," Sammy said and drank his milk.

Out in the car Bronson retrieved his spiral notebook, opened it, and wrote down Dolly Secrist. *Knew I was coming. Claims did not give Weeks my name. First says she read in the paper I was retired. Later says Weeks told her I retired. Babysitting for a month. Couldn't have followed me from Dallas. Knows something. Cannot figure out what.*

He closed the notebook and returned it to his shirt pocket.

Why Casey Had to Die

As he drove up Highway 191 toward the Sun Lodge, Bronson replayed his visit to Dolly's house. Some bit of information jumped at him, but he couldn't quite grasp it.

Chapter 8

As soon as Bronson pulled into the Lodge's parking lot, he noticed the 1956 Chevy parked in the lot. He once again retrieved his notebook, jotted down the tag number, whipped out his cell, and called Michael Hoover. Back in Dallas, his desk had been two away from Bronson's. The phone rang twice before Hoover picked it up. "Missing Persons. Hoover speaking."

"Hey, Hoover. How's it goin'?"

A second of silence followed while Hoover made the connection. "Bronson, is that you?"

"Sure enough."

"I knew it! You wouldn't be able to stay away more than a month. I just won me fifty bucks." Bronson heard Hoover speak to his co-workers. "Hey guys. Bronson's on line two. Pay up. You owe me." A few seconds later, he spoke to Bronson. "Now that I'm richer, what can I do for you?"

"Actually, I need to cash in on a favor."

"Sure, buddy, anything for you, especially now that you've made me richer."

"I need for you to give me a ten-twenty-eight and a ten-twenty-nine." Bronson gave him the license number.

"You think the car with that tag number is stolen?"

"No reason to think so. I'm just checkin' all angles."

A brief silence followed before Hoover asked, "Are you okay?"

Bronson removed his glasses and rubbed the bridge of his nose. Was he okay?

"Talk to me. I don't like this silence."

Bronson detected a note of concern in his colleague's voice. "Carol and me, we've started on our grand United States tour. We're in Safford, Arizona. What could possibly be wrong?"

"Correct me if I'm mistaken, but it seems to me that you're out there in Safford and you've got yourself involved with some crime. Am I in the right ball park?"

"Nah, Hoover. There's been no crime committed."

"Then why the license check?"

"You always did ask a lot of questions."

"And you always avoided answering them." Bronson heard the shuffling of papers. "Shit. Hey, listen. Garza's heading my way. Call you with the information as soon as I can."

Bronson thanked him and hung up. He called the lab next, but Paul was unavailable. Bronson slammed the phone shut. If he were still a detective, he wouldn't be having trouble gathering the information. Frustration gnawed at him, he headed toward the motel. As he walked past the registration desk, he heard someone call his name.

Bronson turned to face the young man behind the counter. "Mr. Bronson, I have a message for you." He handed him a note.

Bronson thanked him and sucked in his breath. The handwriting told him S had not written this one. He let his air out.

The note asked Bronson to stop by Room 205 at his earliest convenience. The signature read L'ee Chalmers, a name Bronson recognized. Her signature had been above the chairperson blank on the contract he signed. It would certainly benefit him to talk to her.

Bronson knocked on the door and to his surprise he heard

a sultry voice say, "Come in."

Bronson reached for the doorknob and opened the door with the full intention of reprimanding L'ee Chalmers for not using any safety precautions. Anybody could have walked in and with a voice like that, she—

Bronson stopped.

Before him sat a very large woman whom Bronson estimated weighed somewhere in the vicinity of three hundred and fifty pounds. She smiled at Bronson and her cheeks bulged ruddily. "Detective Bronson, I presume."

"Ma'am." He bowed his head slightly.

"You must excuse me for not standing up to greet you, or even for not opening the door, but as you can see, that would take a lot more energy than I have."

"No need to fret, Ms. Chalmers."

"That's Mrs." Her hand reached for the wedding ring on a chain around her neck. Her thumb and index finger stroked it and her eyes glassed, perhaps reliving another time, another place. She sighed and her entire body shook. "I can't wear the ring anymore." She looked at her chubby fingers that looked like short, stubby sausages.

Bronson walked over and sat on the bed. "Mrs. Chalmers, eh? Any relation to the Texas senator?"

"Oh, how I wish, Detective Bronson. How I wish." Her eyes twinkled.

Bronson smiled. He wouldn't mind being related to the senator. Women considered him a hunk, his leadership abilities impressed everyone, and more than likely he was destined for the White House. But more important, Texas blood flowed through his veins.

"I'd like to clear one misconception, Ms.—huh, Mrs. Chalmers."

"Call me 'L'ee'." She pronounced it *el-ee*.

50

"Oh really? That is an unusual way of pronouncing your name."

L'ee wiggled in her chair, and the double chins that came in pairs down her throat jiggled. "Of course it is. It's unique. I like being different."

Bronson could see that. Underneath all those rolls of fat lived a beautiful woman.

"So tell me, Detective Bronson, what misconception did you want to clear?"

"I'm no longer a detective. I'm now a private citizen."

"Of course I knew that, but you must forgive me. There's something about you that says *detective*. Maybe it's the way you stare at things, as though absorbing every detail. Your voice. Your composure. It all says *detective*. I can't look at you and not think detective."

She smiled and Bronson felt himself being absorbed by those glittering, stone-gray eyes. Bronson would bet his reputation that sometime in her past, she had turned more than one man's head. "Seems that you're not the only one who thinks this way, ma'am. Reckon I'll always be stuck with that title."

"And does that bother you?"

"Oh, no, ma'am. I reckon I kinda like it."

"Good to hear that, and now that we've cleared the air about our names and titles, I invited you here so that I could answer any questions you may have about the conference." She rested her palms on her lap and the excess rolls of fat in her arms hung down like a wrinkled parachute.

"Do the people who come to this—huh, conference, mystery show, whatever you want to call it—are they always the same people year after year?"

"The majority are. Naturally, we always have some new ones each year and then, of course, there are those who for some reason or other can't make it each year. But the majority, yes, they're repeats. Why would you ask that?"

"There's a couple. He's tall, lean. He and his wife drive a restored 1956 Chevy. Would you by any chance know whom I'm talkin' about?"

"No, sorry. I spend most of my time in the room. I have no idea who drives what and as for 'tall and lean' . . ." She pouted as though trying to place them. Slowly, she shook her head. "We have a lot of tall and lean attendees. Why would you want to know that?"

"Can you think of anybody who might be able to answer my question?"

"Balthasar, perhaps?"

"Who?"

"Balthasar." She giggled. "That's not his real name, of course, but that's what I affectionately call him. Are you familiar with the name Balthasar?"

"Might you be alluding to Romeo's faithful servant?"

L'ee made an elongated face of surprise. "I'm impressed. A detective who actually reads Shakespeare."

"Yes, ma'am. Imagine that. It happens occasionally. So tell me about Balthasar."

"He's my faithful servant. He takes me wherever I need to go. He buys me whatever I need—with my money, of course. But he takes good care of me. He's my companion, my buddy. And I pay him very well."

"And where can I find this Balthasar?"

"He's out on a break. He'll be back shortly, and again I ask, why is this important?"

"Amazin' the things we consider important."

"Yes, indeed. Do you have any more questions?"

Bronson looked at his watch and stood up. "My Carol must be lookin' for me just about now. Best if I be goin'."

"Detective?"

Bronson stopped and looked at L'ee.

"Do you ever answer any questions?"

Bronson smiled and walked out, but not before he saw L'ee throw her arms up in the air.

Chapter 9

Before heading back to his room, Bronson went to the reception area where he knew the contestants had already begun to gather. As the elevator opened and Bronson stepped out, he noticed that people had congregated in separate clusters. They wore their badges announcing them as A Slayer Detective. Under that, the participant's name appeared, and in smaller letters, the city and state from which he came.

Since Bronson's badge rested safely on top of the dresser back in his room, he knew he could move among them undetected. Once he put on the badge, he would probably be bombarded with questions from the eager participants.

No, it'd be best to do this without the badge. Move from group to group. Surely, someone will know the Chevy Man's identity, or even better, he'd encounter the Chevy Man himself.

Bronson headed for the coffeepot and fixed himself a cup. He tasted the coffee. Average. Oh well, at least it was free. Holding on to his cup, he walked around the room in a counterclockwise direction. He studied each man and just as quickly dismissed him. None was the one Bronson searched for. Bronson moved on and continued his search.

Five minutes later, Bronson spotted the Chevy Man, standing by the window, cradling a drink, and smiling at what one of the women in the group said. Bronson approached, not quite sure what he planned to say.

He didn't need to have bothered. Chevy Man looked up and locked eyes with Bronson.

Bronson read Chevy Man's badge. Now he had a name to attach to the Chevy Man: Tom O'Day.

O'Day nodded a small acknowledgment. "Detective, come join us."

Aha. Just as Bronson suspected. Tom O'Day, alias Chevy Man, knew him. Interesting.

The members of the group turned to stare at Bronson.

O'Day pointed at Bronson. "Folks, I'd like you to meet Detective Bronson from Dallas."

"Dallas?" The brunette who had moved to make space for him spoke up first. Her hair was drawn back in a bun that made her face look thin. She had wide brown eyes and a rich, wide smile. Her badge read Gerri Balter. "You're far away from home. Used to be this group was strictly all Arizona, but now we got people coming from the surrounding areas as well. Welcome to our group, Mr. Bronson."

Surrounding areas—Dallas? She must live in a world with very unusual maps. "Thank you, ma'am."

"Did Tom say you're a detective?"

Before Bronson could answer, O'Day stepped forward. "Yes, I did. Allow me to add one more bit of information to the introduction. Detective Harry Bronson is our new consultant."

"Our consultant?" Gerri arched her eyebrows. "Whatever happened to Max? He's been our consultant for years."

The woman next to O'Day—the one Bronson recognized as O'Day's wife, stepped forward. Up until now, Bronson hadn't noticed how delicate her features were, like a porcelain doll's. Her badge identified her as Marie O'Day. "You mean you haven't heard? He was the victim of a hit-and-run accident."

Gerri gasped. "How horrible. Is he all right?"

"Hardly. He's dead," O'Day said.

The smallest woman in the group stepped around the O'Days and faced Bronson. He wondered why he hadn't noticed her before. She wore a tight, bright, lime-green short dress and sparkly dinner rings on each finger. Bracelets of various shapes and widths covered almost half of her lower arm. Bronson could see she was a pretty woman, but from his point of view, she wore a bit too much makeup and showed a bit too much skin.

When she spoke, she addressed the group, but stared at Bronson. "Before we go much further, I think we need to put this in perspective. Don't you agree, Detective Bronson?" She pronounced the word *detective* as though it had turned to mud in her mouth.

The way that she glared at him, the way she confronted him made Bronson feel as though he'd been caught taking a peek in the ladies' locker room. He shifted his weight and looked at her badge. "Katherine, ma'am. I'm not exactly sure what I'd be agreeing to."

Katherine Shephard squinted and frowned.

Tom placed his hand on her shoulder. "Now, Katherine, there's no need to cause any commotion." As she pivoted, the glass she held in her hand sloshed liquid onto the floor. She faced Tom. "You don't think murder is a reason to cause commotion?" Her harsh tone caused others to turn and stare. She placed her free hand on her hip. "Well, I do. Besides, I'm a Texas gal, and I have the right to speak my mind." She turned once more so that now she faced Bronson. "So tell us, Detective Bronson, how long did you know Max before his tragic accident?"

"Never had the pleasure of meetin' him, ma'am."

She finished her drink and set it down. "Oh really?"

Yes, really. "What is it that you're tryin' to say?"

Katherine threw her arms up in the air. "I love it. I absolutely love it. That innocent act is so becoming—and so fake."

Once more Tom placed his arm on Katherine's shoulder and gently pushed her back. "Now, Katherine, please, don't do this."

"Why not? You don't think these people have a right to know about Max's murder?" By now several people had abandoned their groups and a small circle of speculators had gathered around them.

"Katherine, Tom's right," Marie said.

"Fine, but let me just make one point." Before either of the O'Days could stop her, Katherine plunged on. "Your position as a consultant here is a highly desirable one. There's a long waiting list of people who would be thrilled to fill that opening. So how long was your wait, Detective Bronson?" Katherine's eyes became narrow slits in her face.

"You can drop the title, ma'am. It's just Bronson. I'm no longer with the police department, and the organization contacted me about the position. So I was never on any waitin' list."

"With a waiting list of over thirty people, they call you and offer you the job." Katherine snapped her fingers. "Just like that."

"Just like that." Bronson snapped his fingers.

"Hmm, how fortunate for you."

"What can I say? It must have been my lucky star."

"And where was that lucky star when the police department fired you?"

Bronson felt his hands restless and dry. His nerves screamed with tension. She obviously had her own agenda and Bronson aimed to uncover its purpose. He took a step back and glared at Katherine.

Bronson's gaze went to Gerri. "You were fired?" Gerri asked.

"I retired, ma'am, but let's just say it wasn't a completely voluntary retirement."

"Point made." Katherine stormed off and several people followed her, apparently eager to get the scoop.

"I must apologize for my cousin," Marie said. "She's from the heartland of Texas where people believe in speaking their minds."

"Even if their minds are wrong?"

"You're a Texan, Detective Bronson. You should know Texans are never wrong." Marie smiled and winked, her eyes glowing with an inner light.

"I'll file that bit of information away. You never know when it'll be useful."

Tom smiled. "Allow us to introduce ourselves. We haven't met formally. I'm Tom O'Day." He pointed to his right. "And this lovely lady is my wife, Marie. We're from Scottsdale." He pointed to the only other person in the group. "And of course, you've met Gerri Balter from Tucson."

Bronson shook hands with each member. "And the little Texas tornado is . . ."

Marie threw her head back and laughed. "A Texas tornado. I like that. That describes her to a T." She watched her for a few minutes. Katherine, surrounded by people, spoke amiably. "That's my cousin, Katherine Shephard. She's got a heart of gold and a very unique point of view. She really didn't mean anything by what she said."

"Thing is, I'm not sure what she said. Does she think I killed this Max person in order to be your consultant?"

"She never said that."

No, she hadn't, but somehow she had planted that seed and others had been listening and now they talked to Katherine. Bronson switched his attention from Katherine back to Marie. "Do you know any of the details centered around Max's death?"

"Other than that it's an unsolved hit-and-run, no one knows much." Marie finished her drink and handed the glass to a waiter who gathered the empty glasses. "You forget, Detective Bronson, that this is a group of wanna-be detectives. We're here to solve a fake murder, but wouldn't it be much more fun to solve a real one?" Before Bronson could answer, Tom wrapped his arm around his wife and led her away.

Gerri watched them walk away. "Don't worry, Detective Bronson, no one can possibly believe you had something to do with Max's death just so that you could land this job. Although it is interesting that you were never on the waiting list."

Yes, most interesting, Bronson thought and realized he hadn't asked Tom any of the questions that had been screaming for an answer.

S ordered a rum and Coke and inwardly smiled. Word about Bronson's possible involvement in Max's death spread through the room faster than an all-consuming fire. This pleased *S*. The seeds of doubt had been planted among the conference attendees.

Things definitely moved at a faster pace than anticipated. Plans might have to be changed, would probably have to be sped up. That was good. Definitely good.

Without leaving the bar, *S* scanned the room, spotting the people selected to die. That sure was too bad. Most were rather nice. But it was something that needed to be done.

After all, Bronson had to be destroyed.

Chapter 10

Carol grabbed Bronson's arm and led him out of the motel room. "Do you think they'll have steak and eggs on the menu?"

We do in the camper. "Most places usually do. You sure you wouldn't want to whip some up in the camper? We can run the generator."

The elevator door opened and they stepped in. "Silly. We're on vacation. Why would I want to cook?"

"My question precisely." Bronson's attitude brightened. They headed toward the restaurant and there, they'd have good coffee.

While they waited for the hostess to seat them, several people glared at Bronson, then quickly looked away. One table filled with conference attendees leaned toward each other and while staring at Bronson, exchanged whispered words.

Amazing what damage gossip could cause. The rumor had spread faster than the Internet. If he could only find a way to market its speed, he would surely become a millionaire. He inwardly shrugged. Gossip had never really bothered him. For all he cared, they could throw him as many dirty looks as they wanted, so long as they didn't throw him any fingers.

Minutes later, the Bronsons sat down. Immediately Bronson moved his cup so that the waitress could easily fill it.

While she poured Bronson his coffee, Carol turned her cup upside down. "Lowfat milk for me, please." The waitress nodded and left.

Bronson poured two heaping spoonfuls of sugar and was about to pour the third when he caught Carol's stern look. He pushed the sugar container away and instead drowned his coffee with milk.

The waitress returned a few minutes later with Carol's drink. Carol ordered steak and eggs and Bronson requested another cup of coffee, eggs over-easy, bacon well done, and wheat toast.

Throughout the meal, Carol's constant chatter intrigued Bronson. How could anyone find so much to talk about, he wondered. Ah, that was the charm of this woman.

Bronson stared into her sparkling jewel eyes and felt as though he was the luckiest man alive.

"So what do you think about my day's plans?" Carol wiped her mouth and pushed her empty plate away. She looked at him, as though expecting an answer. She frowned. "Harry Bronson, you weren't listening to me."

Bronson scratched his forehead. He had been listening although his thoughts had strayed for just a second. Just his luck she'd catch him at exactly that second. "I was just thinkin' how lovely you look."

Carol smiled. "Flattery will get you everywhere, so I'll repeat myself. I said that I was leaving. I'll be back around five to check about dinner."

Bronson couldn't imagine what she'd be doing until five. He was afraid to ask. He should have listened. He smiled and nodded. She stood up and kissed his lips.

"Enjoy the conference."

Bronson glanced around. Angry, curious eyes stared back. "Oh yeah. It's goin' to be a doozie."

Carol looked at him, squinted as though considering whether she should ask him what he meant. She shrugged and walked away.

Bronson added some sugar to his coffee.

Bronson stood outside of the conference room, listening as the murmur of voices rose with anticipation. The room buzzed with people and almost every seat was occupied.

Bronson swallowed hard, braced himself, and stepped in. A group of women glanced his way then turned their backs on him.

Oh yeah, this promised to be one hum-dinger of a conference.

"Hello, Detective Bronson."

Bronson turned toward the source of the voice.

Gerri smiled up. "I saved you a seat. Come on over and join us."

"Us?"

"Same group as last night. Me, the O'Days, and Katherine. Also, a couple of others you haven't met." Gerri grabbed his arm and pulled him toward the group. "This orientation meeting always begins promptly at nine." She glanced at her watch. "We better hurry."

They barely reached their seats when he spotted L'ee—*el-ee*, Bronson reminded himself although he found it amusing that everyone else pronounced her name the normal way. He watched her waddle toward the stage and noticed that her dress fit her like a tent. When she reached the steps leading to the stage, she leaned on her cane. Her effort to walk toward the stage had taken its toll. She inhaled deeply before ascending each of the four steps.

At the top of the stairs, she gulped in more air. Gradually the room grew silent as she reached for the microphone. "Hi. For those of you who don't know me, I'm L'ee

Chalmers, organizer of the Slayers Mystery Week. Welcome, everyone."

The audience broke into a thunderous combination of clapping and cheering.

L'ee raised her arms and the group slowly grew silent. "Looking around the room, I see a lot of familiar faces. Most of you have been attending this conference forever."

Ripples of small laughter broke among the audience. Some pointed to one another. Others patted themselves on the back.

"But I also see some new faces." She stretched her arms out to show the expanse of the audience. Her arms, Bronson noticed, had the wrinkled softness of partly deflated balloons. "For the benefit of our new attendees, this is the part where we introduce you to our characters. You may or may not take notes. For your convenience, a notebook and a pen have been provided for you in your registration packet." She paused and smiled, her plump face causing her eyes to squeeze shut.

"Speaking of new faces, there is one particular person I'd like to introduce." She stopped, looked down, and bowed her head. When she looked back up, her stone-gray eyes glittered with teardrops. "We all knew . . . and loved . . . Max Iles." She cleared her throat. "He, huh . . . he's . . ." She looked away from the audience, up toward the ceiling. "He's no longer with us. If we could, please, have a moment of silence for our dear Max."

Bronson didn't have to look around to know that questioning eyes stared at him. Did these people really think he ran over Max so he could get this job? The idea, so unconceivable to him, made him wonder why these people would even entertain such an idea. Maybe he should address the issue and squelch the gossip before it blossomed into a force capable of destroying him, not that it hadn't already.

63

Or maybe he should ignore it.

L'ee's coarse voice broke the silence. "Even though filling Max's shoes will be a tremendous responsibility, we are lucky to have a very good replacement. Ladies and gentlemen, I'd like to introduce you to our new consultant, Detective Harry Bronson, formerly of the Dallas Police Department. Detective Bronson, please stand up."

Bronson stood and the silence swallowed him like a large carnivorous monster. Beside him, Gerri clapped and soon others joined in. After a subdued, polite clap, the room returned to its former silent mode. Bronson quickly sat and flashed Gerri a grateful smile.

That went well, he thought.

Up on the stage, a curious frown covered L'ee's face. She shifted her massive weigh as she shuffled some papers. "Uh . . . let's . . . uh . . ." She cleared her throat and using a brighter, happier tone she said, "Let's get the conference rolling."

A thunderous clap broke out.

Bronson found it hard to believe that this crowd was the same one as that of a moment ago.

"Ladies and gentlemen, our cast of characters." She swept the air with her arm and waddled off the stage.

Chapter 11

A stately, middle-aged woman stepped onto the stage. "My name is Ann Nare. I have—had—the most beautiful little girl you've ever seen." She took a tissue out and dabbed her eyes. "You would have loved her, my little angel. My Annie. She was gorgeous and smart. Oh, so smart. In fact, she graduated from high school when she was only sixteen." She paused and wiped more tears away. "Like any mother, I wanted to protect my little girl. So I sent her to private schools from kindergarten all the way through high school. But what good did that do?" Her voice broke and she stopped.

Bronson sat up straighter. His sixth sense—the detective in him—kicked in.

"She went away to college," Ann continued. "Naturally, I wanted her to stay here in town at least the first year or so, but she always dreamed of going to Dallas. And off she went. She never came back."

Bronson wet his lips, scooted to the edge of the chair, and listened intently.

Ann stepped to the side and a young man entered the stage. "I'm David Palmers." He swung his hand in a wide arc, signifying the area around him. "And this is my fraternity." As he walked around the stage, he held his head high and looked around him. "She died here, you know." He shook his head, as though remembering. "That Annie Nare. She was a wild one. It was our annual pledge party. By then we had already made up our minds who we would induct, and who we wanted nothing to do with. Annie came to the party with one of the pledges—Henry Allegri." David smirked. "Good ol' Henry. He certainly wasn't pledge material, but he was dating Annie and that earned him a couple of points. He wanted in so badly, he'd pass Annie around to all the guys."

David walked toward the front of the stage and pointed to the floor. "Right here. That's where it happened." He looked at the audience, then continued, "By the time Henry and Annie got here, she was already stoned out of her mind. Drug overdose is what killed her. Hate to say this, but she brought this on herself. She O.D'd. It's as simple as that." He shrugged and stepped toward the back of the stage.

Bronson kept his gaze glued on the speaker, wishing he could stop this mockery. Instead he wrote down, *Check on fraternity president.* Bronson watched as another young man— this one small in size, wearing thick eyeglasses and clothes that probably were one size too big approached the stage. He stopped, not quite in the center of the stage.

He attempted to smile but all he succeeded in doing was to make his lips tremble. He looked around him as though making sure no one, except the audience, could hear him. "I'm Henry Allegri, and it's true. I'm the one who took Annie to the fraternity party. She was really looking forward to it." He paused as though remembering Annie. A small, sad smile spread across his lips. "You see, Annie had always been sheltered. This was to be her first real party, and look what happened." He looked up at the ceiling and his lips trembled. "Knowing she was so innocent, so pure, I should have watched her more carefully. I guess she bought some drugs, and they were bad or too much for her. She died that night. I should have stayed by her side all night." He lowered his head, shook it, and stepped back.

Bronson saw a group of overgrown boys climb up onto the stage. He knew these would be the fraternity pledges and members, and he knew exactly what they would say.

The one in the center picked himself to be the group's voice. "Hey! We're from Alpha Kappa Lambda." The guys behind him hooted and hollered their support. They moved their arms up and down as though lifting weights. The leader quieted them, then turned to the audience. "We all liked Annie and felt sorry for that jerk of a boyfriend of hers. All Allegri wanted was to be inducted, but we don't take people like him, you know what I mean?" The group behind him made gestures that indicated Henry Allegri was either gay or a loser.

The leader continued, "No way we'd let him in, so he promises us Annie if we induct him. Now Annie—she was a real looker and a bit on the innocent side. That made her real appealing. Some of the guys claimed they already scored with Annie, so by the time Annie and Henry got to the party, we all know her. So Henry sticks to her all night, you know, like glue. Wants to make sure he gets inducted first.

"Man, was he pissed when he found out he didn't make it. He was in the middle of having a conniption fit when some chick screamed. She pointed to Annie, there on the floor. Dead. Poor Annie." The fraternity men lowered and shook their heads and stepped back.

Bronson tensed, like a lamb in a den of lions. He forced himself to take deep breaths and watched a middle-aged man take center stage.

"Reid is the name. Fred Reid. I'm the detective in charge of the case. I'm a bit tense. I just got promoted. My accomplishments in the field of patrol are legendary, so I was booted up. So here I am. It's my first case, and I've got to make it count. I solve it and I'll probably be up for another promotion. So I'll do my best to capture the sick bastard who did this to a pure, innocent girl. Drugs have no place in my city. That's a guarantee."

The curtain closed and thunderous applause broke out around Bronson. L'ee hobbled toward the podium and began to explain the rules of the game.

Bronson stopped listening. He leaned back on his chair and kept his gaze glued on the curtain as though he could find the answers written within the folds of the material.

His mind roared as shock gave way to certainty, for the story Bronson had just heard was Casey's story. The only difference between the actual case and the one that had just been presented was that the names had been changed. Otherwise, everything else matched. This had been his first assignment.

His first failure.

Bronson had always felt that Moises—Casey's boyfriend who had been found guilty of her murder—had been telling the truth about his innocence. Unfortunately, Moises was no longer around to defend himself. He had been conveniently killed in a prison riot. That had prompted Bronson to reopen the case, but those higher up in command had demanded that Bronson drop it. Case was closed and sealed. Forever to be forgotten.

But not by him, and obviously not by whoever was playing this game with him.

Now, more than ever, Bronson felt the need to clear the dead man's reputation and discover S's identity. Bronson became a man possessed and the determination he felt became a red-hot poker inside him, burning him and turning his blood to steam.

Chapter 12

Bronson watched as a group of conference attendees gathered around L'ee. These were probably the novices, the ones who weren't here last year. Bronson memorized their faces.

"So what do you think?"

Bronson turned toward the source of the voice. "I found it a fascinating case. Katherine, isn't it?" Bronson remembered how this little Texas tornado had planted the seed in each of the attendees' brains that he had killed Max in order to obtain this position. Was she part of *S*'s game?

"It is." When Bronson frowned, she added, "Katherine. You asked if that's my name. It is."

"Ah." He looked at her. "What about you, ma'am? What did you think of the case?"

"Best we've had."

"And why's that?"

"The setting. Naturally. Texas. Can't get better than that."

"The previous games—"

Katherine rolled her eyes. "Investigations."

"Yes, of course, investigations. Have any of them ever been set in Texas?"

Katherine shook her head. "Not that I can remember. Far as I know, they all have been set here in Arizona."

"Then why the change this year?"

Katherine shrugged. "Beats me. Guess you'll have to talk to the organizers about that."

"And they are?"

"You'll want the head honcho. That'll be Ms. L'ee, of course." Katherine squinted as though formulating an idea. "It just dawned on me. You're from Dallas, aren't you?"

"I am."

"I wonder if that's a hint. Do you think it's possible that the detective on the script had something to do with Annie's death?"

In this case, anything is possible. "It is an interestin' theory."

"Yeah, no shit. I think I'm going to follow up on that. See ya, sweetie." She winked, turned, and walked away.

Sweetie? First she accuses me of murder and now she's flirting with me? Amazing. Bronson kept his gaze glued on Katherine until she disappeared into the crowd. When he could no longer see her, Bronson turned his attention to the group surrounding L'ee. He recorded brief descriptions and approximate ages. When the last of the stragglers left, he approached L'ee.

L'ee's wide smile bordered on the seductive side. "Detective, good to see you." Her eyes danced with good cheer.

"Likewise, ma'am."

L'ee tilted her head, ever so slightly. For the moment, Bronson forgot she carried a couple of hundred pounds extra. "You're going to have your hands full with this group," she said. "They're so inquisitive."

"Reckon that's the nature of the game."

"Investigation, please, Detective. You want to turn this group against you real fast, you call it a game."

Turn the group against me? Wasn't it too late for that? "Pardon me, ma'am, I meant to say investigation."

L'ee nodded and through the layers of excess fat, Bronson

saw a beautiful shining face. The image lasted but a second, like a camera snapping a picture.

"Now that the investigation is officially on, do you have any last-minute questions?"

"I do. I'd like to know where the scenarios for these conventions come from."

L'ee turned to stare at Bronson. "Most unusual question. Max never asked that."

"What can I say? I'm just a curious little boy."

L'ee smiled and shook her head as though the concept of Bronson ever being or having been a little boy was the most ridiculous thing she'd ever heard. "Six to eight months before each convention is held, we begin to receive manuscripts. We read them, choose the best one, and that's the one that's presented."

"And who authored this year's winner?"

L'ee shrugged. "So that there's no favoritism shown, all manuscripts are sent anonymously. No one, except for the author himself or herself, knows who wrote it."

"Is there any way to find out?"

"Of course. We always acknowledge the creator. At the end of the conference, when the awards are presented, we ask the author to come up to the stage and receive his or her award."

"Wouldn't that put the author at an advantage when solvin' the crime?"

"Not really. The author simply takes himself out of the race."

"So to find him, all I have to do is find the one participant who isn't participatin'."

"Basically, yes, but it's not that simple."

"And why not?"

"The author pretends to be participating, but doesn't offer any hints or clues. In fact, he'll often set up red herrings for his group and others. If nobody solves the puzzle, the author walks away with the trophy."

Bronson inwardly frowned. He didn't want to wait until the conference was over to find out who authored the script. He had never been good at waiting. In fact, he hated the waiting game . . . huh, investigation. "What about the attendees? Do you have a list of all of the attendees?"

"Yes, of course. Everyone here has to register and pay before he can attend. Why would you want such a list?"

"Actually, I'd rather see their applications."

L'ee's eyebrows furrowed. "What in the world for?"

"One, it keeps me busy. Two, I'll know a bit about the participants, and I'll know how much I can B.S. them."

L'ee's face brightened and her eyes shined with mirth. "Ooooh, Detective Bronson, you're good. You're really going to provide these people with a challenge."

Her teasing manner amused Bronson. This woman truly had charm. "So that means you're goin' to let me see the applications?"

L'ee considered her answer for a moment. "I suppose there's no harm in showing them to you. There's nothing really private there, except maybe for their addresses and phone numbers."

"I promise, ma'am, that I won't visit them or make any obscene calls." He raised his two fingers showing her the Boy Scout's pledge.

L'ee smiled. "The Cactus Room is my temporary office while I'm here at the convention. You'll find a green file box there. That's where all the applications are. Help yourself."

"Thank you, ma'am. That green box—it has all the applications?"

"Even mine."

"But not mine."

L'ee's eyebrows arched. "You're absolutely right. You should have filled one out. Maybe you can do that while you're there?"

"No problem, ma'am. Is that unusual—that I didn't fill one out?"

"Why of course. Everyone needs to have one. That's what keeps our records straight."

"Ah, paperwork. Don't you just love it?"

"It's not my favorite."

"Nor anybody else's." Bronson tilted his head toward the exit sign. "If you'll excuse me, ma'am, I think I'll head toward the Cactus Room."

"You do that. Don't forget to fill out that application form and to make yourself available to our attendees."

That, he planned to do.

Chapter 13

Two items in the applications intrigued Bronson. One blank asked for the number of previous conferences the person had attended. Those that listed three or less, Bronson earmarked.

Going strictly by probability, chances were that whoever was playing this elaborate game with him was not the usual attendee. This was probably his first conference, or his second. Possibly his third.

The other point of interest centered on the applicant's birth date. The application clearly stated that filling in this information was strictly optional. Those who did fill it in would receive a birthday card on their birthday.

Fortunately for Bronson, most applicants not only gave their birth dates, they also gave their birth year. Those who were thirty-eight years or younger, Bronson eliminated as he felt sure the culprit would have to be someone at least in his forties.

Based on the addresses given, Bronson eliminated three more applicants. One stated that she lived in Gallup—had always lived in Gallup—and had only heard about this conference last year.

Another made a similar claim about Phoenix. The third one was a local Safford resident—"born and raised in this God-fearing Mormon town."

That left Bronson with thirty-three possibilities.

Bronson rubbed his forehead. *Thirty-three.* Somehow he'd

have to narrow that list. He tapped his fingers on the application forms. That reminded him, he needed to fill one out.

As he did, he knew something bothered him about it. He took out his notebook and wrote down the word *application.*

Then he copied the names, addresses, and phone numbers of his top thirty-three suspects. He had just finished returning the applications to their original file box when his cell rang.

Bronson looked at the caller I.D. and quickly answered, "Hey, Hoover."

"Hey yourself."

Bronson looked at his watch. He had been locked up with the applications for over two hours. He felt sure L'ee wouldn't like that. "What did you find?"

"What? No hello? How are you? How are things in the Dallas police department? Are things still as messed up as they were when your desk was two away from mine? Whatever happened to manners? Small chitchat, that kind of thing?"

"Sorry, my mind isn't functionin' right."

"Did it ever?"

"Always did. You're thinkin' of your mind."

"At least you're admitting that I have a mind."

"That's somethin'."

"Yeah, and I guess I'll have to settle for that." Hoover cleared his throat. "The car you're looking for, it's a 1956 Chevy?"

"That's the one."

"It's registered to Jackie Lucio. I anticipated your next request, so I gave Paul her name. He's looking her up."

"Paul? Over at the lab? That Paul?"

"Yeah, Paul McKenzie. That Paul. Is there another?"

For a moment, Bronson fell speechless. "Why Paul?"

"He's always had a love affair with computers, but lately, he's really gotten involved with them. I swear, that guy lives and breathes computers. Anyway, he offered to do it. You don't mind, do you?"

"Nah, not at all. I'll give Paul a buzz, but before I do, did the registration form say anythin' about either Tom or Marie O'Day?"

"Not that I remember. Want me to check out the names for you?"

"I'm goin' to talk to Paul. I'll see if he wants to do it."

"Oh, he will. He'll jump at the opportunity, and he'll probably do it a lot faster than I will."

"Thanks, buddy."

"Hey, don't you get mushy on me just cuz you retired."

Bronson smiled and imagined that Hoover was also smiling. "I owe you."

"Big time."

Even though Hoover couldn't see him, Bronson nodded. He knew that before this was over, he would owe a lot of people, especially Michael Hoover and Paul McKenzie.

Bronson thanked his old friend, hung up, retrieved the spiral notebook he carried in his shirt pocket, and added the name Jackie Lucio to the list. Next, he called Paul McKenzie. "Hey, Paul. I hear tell you're into computers," Bronson said once Paul had answered the phone.

"Oh yeah. Gives me something to do and keeps me off the streets."

"So does workin' in the lab."

"True, true, but computers provide a way to spend my time in a relaxed atmosphere."

"Even when it's work related?"

"Specially when it's work related, which reminds me.

You needed information on Jackie Lucio, owner of a 1956 classic?"

"I do."

"You don't mind me asking, what did you get yourself into? This is a sweet little old lady, eighty-seven to be precise. Got one speeding ticket when she was in her twenties and a parking violation in her fifties. That's the extent of her criminal record. What could you possibly want with her?"

"I'm goin' to see if I can make myself an heir and inherit that beauty of a car."

"Nah, I don't think so. Isn't this the same Bronson who drove a broken-down white seventies Ford his entire career?"

"Now you know why I want the Chevy." Bronson heard Paul chuckle. "You did the ten-twenty-nine?"

"If the car's stolen, no one reported it. Is that it? You're looking into a possible stolen vehicle?"

"To be truthful, I'm not quite sure what I'm lookin' for. I'm just coverin' all possible loose ends. Which leads me to the next question. Am I out of favors?"

"Hell, no. The more favors I do for you, the more you'll owe me."

"Great."

"So what's up?"

Bronson retrieved his notebook and quickly scanned his notes. "There's a middle-aged couple from Scottsdale, Arizona. They go by the names of Tom and Marie O'Day. See what you can find and get back to me as soon as possible."

"Yes, sir."

Bronson pictured Paul saluting. "Sorry, didn't mean to order you around."

Paul chuckled. "I'm just kidding, but it sure would be helpful if you gave me a bit more information."

Bronson retrieved his spiral notebook and thumbed

through it until he found the page marked O'Days. "Lucky you, I got their address and their birth date and year."

"That'll make a good beginning. Let me have the info."

Bronson read off the information, thanked him, and hung up. He opened the door wide enough to look down the hall. He certainly didn't want to bump into L'ee. He should have been out there mingling with the crowd instead of being locked up in the room, but since when had he done what he was supposed to? Why start now?

Fortunately, the hallway looked deserted. He stepped out.

"There you are."

Bronson turned to face two elderly ladies. He waited for them to join him.

Even before they reached him, the one to the right spoke up. "You know how they told us that drugs caused Annie Nare's death?"

Bronson nodded.

"Is that possible?"

Bronson thought about the question. He realized he didn't understand it. "Is what possible?"

The contestant frowned, telling him that her question was very obvious. "The drugs. Can they really kill you?"

Bronson let out a sigh. It was going to be a three-cups-of-coffee evening.

Chapter 14

By the time Bronson made his way to the coffeepot, he had answered a half dozen or so more stupid questions. Two showed that intelligence thrived in small doses, and one that floored him. Had he still been employed with the police department, he would have recruited this person.

Just as he finished fixing his coffee, he saw Gerri Balter approach. Today she wore her hair down which Bronson thought looked better than in a bun. "May I speak with you?" She smiled at him.

He smiled back. He intuitively liked Gerri. She had been the first to clap at today's meeting when L'ee introduced him. She had saved him a place in the crowded room. Whenever he saw her, she carried a warm smile on her lips. "What can I do for you, ma'am?"

"We need to come up with some kind of strategy."

"To solve this case, you mean?"

Gerri's eyebrows shot up all the way to her hairline. "No, that would be cheating. You're our consultant. You're not allowed to give us any ideas. All you can do is answer questions."

"Glad to see you're not the cheatin' kind."

Gerri's smile broadened.

"So what kind of strategy are you talkin' about?"

Gerri hesitated. "I'm not quite sure how to phrase this, but there are some rumors floating around." She looked down at the floor.

"Ah, I see where this is leadin'. Some of these people think I killed Max so I could have his job."

Relief flooded Gerri's face. "Oh, then you know."

"Yes, ma'am. There's nothin' to these rumors, you know?"

Gerri's eyes widened. "I never thought—not even for a second—you had anything to do with Max's death." She made a sweeping motion with her arm. "But these people don't think like I do. We need to convince them you're innocent."

"Why is this so important to you?"

"I just don't think it's right, being accused like that, talking behind your back. I tell everyone what a ridiculous idea that is. Wish there was a way we could talk to a mass of them, convince them. Then they can help spread the word."

Talk to a mass of them. That would be perfect. "Actually, ma'am, there is."

Gerri tilted her head making her look like a bird on watch. "Oh?"

"You and I—we've been thinkin' along the same lines. I was figurin' maybe I could host a reception. Kind of like 'Meet Your New Consultant' get-together. Naturally, I couldn't invite everyone. So we tell them we did a random drawin'. Their names were selected. I think if we hold it down to thirty-three names, that would be a good number."

She squeezed her features together, making her look comical. "That's a nice even number."

"Yes, ma'am, it is."

"Why thirty-three? Why not thirty or thirty-five?"

"Thirty-three is my lucky number."

"I see." She nodded. "Anyway, I think I like your idea. I know the Events Coordinator. I bet I can talk him into providing a room for our gathering. I'll even see if L'ee has enough money to supply some fruit and vegetable trays. We can have an open bar where everyone buys his or her own drinks. That'll bring the hotel some money which will guarantee that Wayne Weeks will provide the room. How does that sound?"

"Sounds like you've gotten it all worked out. You sure you wouldn't mind setting this up for me?"

"No, not at all. I'll get right on it. I brought my laptop with me. I can generate invitations and pass them around."

"Why don't you make the invitations, then give them to me, and I'll pass them out? You've got enough to do."

"Are you sure?"

"Of course."

"But how would you know who to invite?"

"I'll make sure the Little Texas Tornado—Ms. Katherine Shephard—is there. And I'll invite the O'Days, Tom and Marie. Also, L'ee. You, of course. The rest will be names I draw from the applications. Only fair way to do it." The only information he kept to himself was that he already knew which thirty-three conference attendees he would invite.

Bronson watched as Gerri trotted away, eager to make the arrangements. He felt bad, almost as if he was using her, which he wasn't. Not really. She had been thrilled to help. Perhaps a bit too thrilled.

Bronson wondered why and made a notation about it in his spiral notebook.

Chapter 15

Bronson spent the next two hours answering questions and helping the conference attendees keep their facts straight. Several times he spotted Tom and Marie O'Day. He slowly worked his way toward them but each time a different conference attendee stopped him, wanting to know this or that.

When he finally found the opportunity to approach them, his cell phone rang. He looked at the caller I.D. It read *Paul McKenzie*. He would take the call.

As he flipped the phone open, he headed away from the crowd. "Hey, Paul."

"Bronson, glad I caught you. I wanted to warn you, watch your back."

Paul's jovial tone normally intrigued Bronson, but this time his all-business voice set Bronson on edge. "Meanin'?"

"Meaning I checked out the O'Days."

"And?"

"The address you gave me, it's a fake. The street exists, but its numbers don't run that high. You told me that they listed Scottsdale as being their place of residency. So I checked for a marriage license. There's none. I expanded my search to all of Arizona. Know what I came up with?"

Bronson rubbed his forehead. He wished Paul would get to the point. "What did you come up with?"

"I got a match."

"Oh?"

"You gave me their birth dates. That produced a mismatch."

What the heck was a mismatch? Is that computer technology?
"Meanin'?"

"Meaning that in all six cases where a Tom O'Day married a Marie O'Day, none of the birth dates listed matched. So those were not the O'Days you're looking for."

"So what you're tryin' to say is that the Tom and Marie O'Day I know do not really exist." *Gee, I could swear they looked real.*

"I even went a step further. I checked Arizona's county records for a birth certificate on Tom O'Day. Couldn't do one on Marie simply because I don't have her maiden name." Paul briefly paused before continuing, "I guess by now you figured I didn't find any. Only thing left to do was do a joint search for Tom and Marie O'Day."

"And of course you found nothin'?"

"No, I did find some O'Days, but not as many as you'd think there would be. There's several Tom O'Days and a bit less Marie O'Days. But when you do a joint search, you come up with a limited number. So I took those names, tried to match them with the birth dates you gave me and cross matched them with the addresses and that's when I came out with nothing."

"Did your computer search come up with anythin' useful?"

"One interesting fact."

Bronson open his spiral notebook and clicked the pen open. "What's that?"

"Back during the days of Butch Cassidy and the Sundance Kid, Tom O'Day was one of the bank robbers who held up the bank in South Dakota along with the Wild Bunch members. Now, there's no relation to the present Tom O'Day, mind you, but it is an interesting fact."

Bronson closed his notebook and placed his palm on his forehead as he shook his head. "Yes, fascinatin'. Think maybe the O'Days could be under the Witness Protection Program?"

"You and I know most of those are in prison under a different name. But is it possible? Yeah, it could be, but there's no way the U.S. Marshal Service would give us that information, and I'm not yet a good enough hacker to get past their firewalls."

"A hacker? You're a hacker?"

"No, not really, but I wouldn't mind pursuing that field."

"Be careful. Remember which side of the law you're on."

"Don't worry. I'd only do it for people like you."

"That's a relief, and I'll keep that in mind, but back to the O'Days. Seems like Tom and Marie O'Day are names they chose for themselves."

"That's my guess."

"I wonder why they didn't bother to build up a history behind their names. What is it that they're hidin'?"

"That's why I called you to warn you to watch your back."

"I'll do that, buddy. Thanks." Bronson closed the cell phone and dropped it in his shirt pocket.

This was turning out to be one heck of a retirement.

Knowing Bronson, Sam couldn't accept the idea that Bronson would host a "Meet Your Consultant Get Together." He had to have a hidden agenda, and trying to figure out what that was drove Sam crazy.

Sam poured a drink and thought some more. No new ideas came to mind. Not that it mattered. So let him host this party. So what? What possible harm could he do?

One thing Sam felt sure about was that Bronson would not

want to involve his precious Carol. But Sam had other plans for her.

Carol would not only be involved, she would become one of the victims.

Sam drank the rest of the drink and smiled. It was time to go meet Carol.

Chapter 16

Bronson watched the drink girl. A pretty thing, no more than in her early twenties. Her job consisted solely of collecting the discarded drinks and taking customers' orders. She looked hurried, frazzled, and a bit disappointed. Seemed like these conference attendees were not the best of tippers.

By now she had her tray full of empty and semi-empty glasses and headed back toward the kitchen.

Bronson stepped in front of her. "I need a favor."

She frowned, but when Bronson showed her the fifty-dollar bill he held in his hand, her eyes lit up. "What kind of favor?"

"There's a couple attending this conference. They can do wonders for my career. So I want to buy them drinks. I want them to think I've done my homework, and I'm willin' to please them. I would like for you to find out what they're drinkin', then bring me their drinks and I'll give them to them." He glanced over at the O'Days and noticed that Katherine Shephard had joined them. "Make that three drinks. If you do that for me, here's the fifty to cover the cost of the drinks. The rest is for you to keep."

"That's all you want?"

"Actually, there's one more thing."

She frowned.

Bronson continued, "I do this great trick that I know will

impress them, but I need three bags. Think you can bring me three large bags, too? Preferably plastic bags."

"The bags and the drinks. That's all?"

Bronson nodded.

The drink girl slowly smiled. "Which three people are you talking about?"

Bronson pointed them out. He watched as the drink girl headed toward them and took their orders. She headed for the bar and returned a few minutes later carrying a tray with three drinks and the plastic bags.

She started to hand him the tray, then hesitated. "You're not going to put anything in their drinks, are you?"

Bronson shook his head. "You've been watchin' too much T.V. No, I'm not goin' to do that. All I plan to do is give them their drinks and show them a magic act."

"And the change from the fifty is mine?"

"And the change is yours."

She handed him the tray. "The gentleman has the Coke. The lady, the Sprite. The hot dish has the margarita. You have the three baggies."

Bronson smiled. "Thank you, ma'am." He accepted the tray and watched the drink girl walk away.

Bronson set the tray down, stuffed the bags in his pocket, took out his handkerchief, and scanned the room. No one seemed to be paying attention to him. Using the handkerchief, he wiped the outside of each glass. He returned his handkerchief to his pocket, picked up the tray, and headed toward the O'Days and Katherine.

"Let me see if I got this right." He looked at Tom. "The Coke is yours."

He nodded.

Bronson's glance shifted toward Marie. "Yours is the Sprite."

"Yes." She reached for it.

Bronson turned to Katherine. "And that means that the margarita must be yours."

"It is, but since when did you get hired to deliver drinks?" Katherine accepted her drink.

Bronson smiled. "Truth is, ma'am, I feel we got started on the wrong foot. So I asked the drink lady to let me pay for your drinks."

Tom looked at his Coke and smiled. "If I'd known you were buying, I would have ordered a mixed drink."

"It's not too late to change."

"Nah, I was just kidding. Thanks for the drinks."

"Maybe we should reciprocate," Marie said. "Can we buy you a drink?"

"I'm a coffee drinker and I just finished a cup. But thanks for the offer. But if you're lookin' to return the favor, there's somethin' you can do."

Tom's eyebrows furrowed. He took a large gulp of his soda. "And what favor is that, Detective Bronson?"

"I'd like a ride in that Chevy of yours. I've always loved vintage cars and yours is the cherry."

Tom and Marie exchanged looks. "The Chevy?" Tom asked.

"Yes, wasn't that you and Marie drivin' that Chevy in Albuquerque? Couldn't help notice. Like I said, cars are a special interest of mine."

"You're very observant." Katherine finished her drink and set the glass down. Bronson memorized its location.

"Reckon that comes from bein' a detective all of these years."

"You were in Albuquerque?" Marie asked.

Bronson nodded. "Yes, Ma'am. But then you knew that."

"Maybe not." Tom set his drink down at the edge of a

planter. "We're ordinary people enjoying a convention." He turned toward his wife. "Are you ready?"

Bronson stepped forward, blocking his way. "What about the Chevy? It's not in the parkin' lot."

Tom glared at him, remained quiet for a moment, then frowned. "For your information, not that it's any of your business, the Chevy does not belong to us and that's why it's not in the parking lot." He tried going around Bronson, but again Bronson blocked his exit.

"Then who does it belong to?"

Tom crossed his arms and glared at Bronson. "Are you investigating us, Detective?"

"Is there a reason I should?" Bronson noted that perspiration beads had formed on Tom's forehead.

"For your information a friend of ours is inheriting the Chevy. His elderly aunt lives in Albuquerque and he lives in Tucson. He couldn't take the time off from work to drive all the way to Albuquerque. We offered to do it for him. We drove to Albuquerque, picked up the car, and yes. While in Albuquerque, we stopped to do the tourist bit. Any other questions?"

"Just one."

Tom's eyes widened, obviously surprised by the answer. "And that is?"

"The elderly aunt's name is—"

"I don't have to give you that information."

"No, you don't, but that's goin' to make me think you're hidin' somethin'." Bronson smiled. "So are you hidin' somethin'?"

Tom's poker face offered no clues. After a brief silence, he said, "Jackie Lucio. L-U-C-I-O." He spoke through almost closed lips. "Now if you'll excuse me, Marie and I have other things to do."

Bronson stepped aside and Tom offered his wife his hand.

She looked down at her drink. She had hardly tasted it. "Let's go," she said. She set her drink next to her husband's.

"Thanks for the drinks," Tom said and both walked away.

Bronson watched them and heard Katherine say, "I think you wasted your money."

Not at all. "Life is hard."

"Life is what you make of it." Her gaze followed one of the conference attendees. "If you'll excuse me, I have a mystery to solve." She ran to catch the man she had been watching.

Bronson took out the plastic bags and picked up a glass by its edge. He dumped the remainder of the drink in the potted plant and dropped the glass inside one of the bags. He did the same with the other two glasses.

Now all he needed was a box large enough to hold all three glasses in their bags and some packing material. He remembered seeing a variety-type store somewhere in the downtown vicinity. He would buy the necessary items, then head off to the post office.

There goes another favor, Bronson thought.

Chapter 17

This was living.

Carol could spend her entire life lying by the pool, absorbing the sun's rays. Well, maybe she wasn't really absorbing the rays. She had read about skin cancer and knew better. She selected a shady area where she could rest and enjoy the fresh air.

No worries. No cares. Just she, the sun—okay, the shade—the fresh air, and a good book.

Ahhh.

Without opening her eyes, she felt something had changed. She sucked in her breath and slowly opened her eyes. She saw a stranger looking down at her.

Shortly after dropping the package off at the post office, Bronson returned to the convention and hoped no one had noticed he was missing. At the rate he was going, he should refuse to accept the thousand-dollar check he would be receiving for being the consultant.

He headed straight for the coffeemaker. He poured himself a cup, added three spoonfuls of sugar, and had just reached for the creamer when he heard someone say, "There you are, Detective Bronson. You are a hard one to find."

Bronson turned and inwardly flinched when he realized it was the same two elderly ladies who always asked stupid questions. "Sorry, I've been makin' the rounds, and we probably missed each other. What can I do for you ladies?" He poured the cream and stirred his coffee.

"We're thinking that maybe Annie wasn't really killed. It's all a fraternity joke–type thing. How can we prove she is really dead?"

Bronson sipped his coffee. "You could demand to see the body."

"No, that won't work. She could be acting and pretend she's dead when she really isn't."

Okay, so maybe he'd keep the thousand dollars. "You'd be able to tell if she was really dead."

"But how?"

"For one, dead people don't breathe. If she wasn't dead, you'd see her chest risin'. She'd have a pulse."

The elderly ladies' faces lit up. "Oh, thank you, Detective Bronson. You're brilliant. We'll try that."

"You do that," Bronson said and felt relieved as he watched them walk away.

His attention quickly shifted from them to the man heading his way. By most people's standards, Bronson had a large, solid build as though he had been carved from a huge, single piece of granite.

However, the man approaching towered above Bronson by a good eight inches and was twice as muscular. That kind of body required daily workouts in a gym. Bronson certainly would never want to encounter him on a dark street. Or even a lit one.

"I understand you wanted to talk to me," the stranger said. Even though he was as bald as an egg, he had bushy eyebrows that hovered over a pair of fierce black eyes.

Bronson searched his mind, trying to place the stranger, but nothing popped up. He must have given the stranger a quizzical look as he said, "I'm Joe Simes."

That didn't help any. "Mr. Simes, how can I help you?"

Simes frowned. "I think, Detective, that you don't know me by my real name. The name Ms. L'ee gave me is Balthasar."

Ah, the faithful servant. "Thanks for clarifyin' that. You're right. I never got your real name."

"Don't feel like the Lone Ranger. I think everyone here at the conference knows me as Balthasar. I don't mind. Makes me feel kind of important." He looked at Bronson's cup of coffee. "Any good?"

"Average, but much better than the one I drink at home. My poor Carol—a great little woman—but she makes a lousy cup of coffee."

Balthasar smiled as he poured himself a cup of coffee. "So what did you want to talk to me about?"

"I spotted a 1956 Chevy in the parkin' lot. I was hopin' you could tell me who it belonged to."

"Sorry, Detective, I would have no idea."

"Can you tell me anything about Tom or Marie O'Day?"

Balthasar took a sip of coffee. "Nothing that would really matter. They're faithful conference attendees. Nice folks."

"Would you say they've attended say, maybe five conferences?"

"Oh no. This conference has been a yearly event for the past ten years. The O'Days are part of our original attendees. Why do you ask?"

"No particular reason. They seem so knowledgeable, but now I see why." Bronson finished his coffee and set the cup down. "Thanks for answerin' my questions."

"No problem."

Bronson turned and walked away. He retrieved his pocket

notebook and thumbed through its pages until he found what he was looking for.

According to their application form, this was the O'Days' first conference.

Chapter 18

Just as Sam finished reading the paper and set it down, the cell rang. The caller I.D. told Sam, Balthasar was on the other end. That couldn't be good news. Balthasar never called. "Is everything okay?"

"I'm not sure. Bronson just asked me about the O'Days."

Damn that Bronson. It was much too soon. "What about them?"

"He wanted to know how many conferences they've attended."

Sam's fingers tapped the dresser with nervous anticipation. "And you told him?"

"Told him they've been attending since the very beginning."

Sam felt the stirrings of anger. *Why did he have to lie?* Sam took in a deep breath before continuing, "Why did you do that?"

"I thought this way he wouldn't investigate them. Like you said, he'll be looking for someone who has never attended before."

Sam formed a fist and continuously hit the air. "Don't ever make the mistake of underestimating Bronson. He acts like he doesn't know anything, but he's a brilliant man. Your lie may have done a lot of damage."

"What do you want me to do?" When he spoke, his words came out as cold as an Alaskan breeze.

"Fix it." Sam matched his cold tone and snapped the cell shut.

Balthasar stared at the phone. Sam had never hung up on him or spoken in anger. That only meant that Sam was feeling the pressure. Good. It was about time.

Balthasar laughed at Sam's orders. He certainly had no intention of "fixing it."

As soon as Carol stepped into the room, she knew her hubby had emerged himself deep into his work. True, he had been hired as a consultant, but had he found a case to work on? Darn him. Would she have to remind him about his retirement—his promise? Couldn't he for once stay away from solving cases? She should have known better.

When he saw her, he immediately closed the pocketsize, spiral notebook and returned it to his shirt pocket. He looked at her and flashed her a you-caught-me-being-a-naughty-little-boy grin.

Normally, that would have made Carol smile. This time she didn't. "What was that?" She pointed to his shirt pocket.

Bronson's hand automatically went to touch his shirt pocket as though reassuring himself the notebook had not vanished. "That? That's my notebook."

"I know that."

"Oh, sorry. I thought you asked."

"I did."

"Then?"

"Harry Bronson, you know exactly what I mean. That's the notebook you always keep with you when you're working on a case. You jot down every single detail, and then spend hours reading your notes until something clicks."

"Sometimes things don't click." He took out the notebook and thumbed through it.

"Like now?"

"Like now."

Carol sighed and focused her eyes on him. "So you are working on a case."

"I've been hired as a consultant, if that's what you mean."

"Is that all it is? Your consultant notes?"

"Mmm." Bronson opened the notebook and began reading the comments he had written. His eyes glazed as he concentrated on what he was reading.

Carol sat down on the bed facing her husband. "I met the most fascinating person today—someone from the conference."

For a long second, Bronson did not respond. Carol cleared her throat. He looked up at her as though he knew he needed to say something. He scratched his chin. "That's nice."

"Want me to tell you about it?"

Relief flooded his face. He looked back down at his notes. "Sure."

Carol slowly shook her head. She could tell him anything, and he wouldn't hear a single word. She had hoped that now that he had retired, this wouldn't happen again. But here he was, deeply involved with his notes, living in a world all of his own. "I met a serial killer today."

Without looking up from his notes, Bronson replied, "That's nice, dear."

"We're going on a killing spree tomorrow."

"Good." He turned the page and frowned. "Hope you enjoy it."

Carol jumped up from the bed. "Harry Bronson!" She placed her hands on her hips. One of these days she would definitely have to give him an award for being the Most Frustrating Man.

Bronson closed his notebook and stuffed it back into his pocket. "What? What did I do now?"

Sam had taken a big risk by meeting Carol face-to-face, but things had worked out just fine. Carol hadn't recognized Sam.

Sam had expected Bronson not to make the connection. After all, so many years had gone by. Carol, on the other hand, could have easily remembered. Women tend to recall the details and remember faces easier than men did.

But neither had made the connection. Neither had recognized Sam.

And that little mistake would cost Carol her life.

Chapter 19

Word had spread rapidly about "The Meet Your Consultant Party," and although thirty-three invitations had been issued, Bronson estimated that at least fifty people attended. That made his job harder. Well, that's the way the cookie crumbles, he thought. But no matter—as long as the right thirty-three attended.

He walked around, looking at name tags. He paused to talk to several people, working into the conversation the word Dallas. He noted their reactions, recorded their comments.

An hour later, he had eliminated twenty-one names. Twelve more to go. Not bad. He mingled some more, deleted seven more possibilities. The numbers had reached a figure he could work with.

He looked around, trying to spot one of the five. From behind him, someone said, "I have a question for you, Detective."

Bronson turned to face a distinguished-looking man in his early to mid-forties. He wore a beige turtleneck and a double knit sports coat. Bronson thought he was overdressed for the occasion and wondered what his background was. Bronson looked down at his badge. It read Trent Powers.

Bronson inwardly smiled. Powers' name was at the top of his list. "What can I do for you, Mr. Powers?"

"You're from Dallas, right?"

"I am."

"So am I."

Bronson had known that. Powers was one of the few who not only lived in Dallas but was also the right age. That combination had caused his name to go to the top of the list along with another attendee, Norman Childes. "That so?"

"Yep. In fact, we've met before."

Bronson searched his mind, but came out blank. "Have we now?"

"I'm hurt. You don't remember me."

"In my line of work, I meet a lot of people."

Powers nodded. "That's understandable." He squinted as though concentrating on what to say next.

Bronson squinted back.

Powers' eyes opened wider in amazement. He shook his head. "There's one thing that's bothered me all of these years about you."

"Just one? I must be improvin'."

Powers didn't laugh. He didn't even smile. He stared at Bronson and after a moment's pause, he continued, "You're a big-city cop. Dallas' favorite. You supposedly always solve the crime. But to me, you come across as a smalltown hick. Why's that?"

"Could be because I was born and raised in Van Alstyne. It's almost a real city now, but while I was grownin' up, the place consisted of no more than a buildin' here and a buildin' there."

"So you are a small-time hick."

"If you say so."

"I have another question."

"You're on a roll. Go ahead."

"Why haven't you told anyone you recognized this case?"

Good thing he played poker. He made sure his features didn't betray him. "Meanin'?"

This time Powers did smile, but the smile contained no humor. "Please give me more credit than that. I was there.

People here are calling the victim Anne Nare, but you and I know her as Casey Secrist." His lips drew back, but the sorrowful eyes shattered the intended smile.

Bronson recognized the smile. It had become a note in his notebook. Trent Powers, a wild, wide-eyed youth. One of the proud members of Alpha Kappa Lambda. "Do you keep up with your fraternity brothers?"

"You lied. You do remember me."

"Seems that way. What can you tell me about your college friends?"

"Not much. We graduated. We went our separate ways. I see the frat president Sydney Stockwell every once in a while, but we're not close. Not even friends. Other than that, the only one I know anything about is Ken."

"That would be Ken Chalmers, Texas senator."

"The one. The only." Powers temporarily paused. He looked away and grinned as though remembering the good times they had. "I don't keep in touch, though. All I know is what I read in the newspapers."

"As much press as he gets, that should keep you busy."

Powers actually smiled. A real smile. "He works hard to get all of that press. He's always been a great leader."

"So why wasn't he your fraternity president?"

"Stockwell's father had been the president. He expected his son to follow in his footsteps. We simply followed tradition and elected Stockwell. But all the guys at the frat house knew Ken Chalmers was the real leader. Even Stockwell followed him. But tradition is tradition."

"Tradition is good." Bronson removed his glasses and squeezed his nose bridge. "How's your writin' comin'?"

Powers' eyebrows arched. "How did you know I like to write?"

"Someone had to write the script for this convention."

Powers nodded. "I see. You think because I recognized the case, I wrote the script?"

"Makes sense to me."

"Sorry to disappoint you, Detective, but I'm not the author. You and I know you wrote it. But why you'd come all the way over here to solve the crime is beyond me."

"Accordin' to all the press, Casey's boyfriend killed her. What would make you think the case isn't solved?"

Something like panic flew across Trent's eyes, but just as quickly as it came, it disappeared. "What else am I supposed to think? You're here and you wrote that script."

"Are consultants allowed to write the scripts?"

Powers shrugged. "Dunno. I'm not familiar with the rules. This is only my first time here."

"Why are you here?"

"I received a flyer in the mail advertising the convention. On the back of the flyer there was an announcement about the contest."

"What kind of contest would that be?"

"You fill out your name, address. That kind of stuff. Send that coupon in. It's probably placed in a box for a drawing. Third place winner receives fifty percent off the conference fee. Second place winner gets a free conference. First place winner gets all expenses paid, including travel allowance."

"And you won first place."

"First and only time I've won anything. Didn't seem right not to accept. So naturally, I claimed my prize."

"Naturally." Bronson spotted the O'Days. He definitely wanted to talk to them. "So when you heard the case presented on stage, didn't it strike you as being rather odd?"

"I knew you were here. I had seen you. I just assumed you wrote it."

"Imagine that."

"Are you telling me you didn't write it?"

"I'm interested in learnin' more about this contest. You already got your money for travel expanses?"

"A Southwest ticket to Tucson came in the mail. A private charter met me there and flew me to Safford. The hotel courtesy van was waiting for me. I take all my meals here. My room's paid for. No exchange of cash. Why do you want to know this?"

"The charter flight—what's the name of the company?"

Powers' eyes danced around as though attempting to picture the airplane. "Don't remember. This man had a sign with my name on it. I approached him. He told me to follow him. He led me to a real small plane. A two-seater. I climbed in. Never noticed the name or even if it did have a name."

"The pilot—what did he look like?"

Powers shrugged. "Average, I guess. Brown hair—or maybe light blond. Average size and build. I dunno. He was just an ordinary guy. Again, I ask. Why do you want to know this? What's going on?"

"Seems like someone went to a lot of trouble to bring you here."

"It was a contest. I won."

"Congratulations."

"What are you saying? The contest was rigged?"

"Can't really say that, can I? First time I've heard of the contest."

"But you don't really think it was legitimate?"

"Didn't say that."

Powers sighed and shook his head. "You're as frustrating now as you were back then. What is it exactly that you're trying to say?"

"I'd watch my back, if I were you." *Provided that you are*

tellin' the truth. But if you're lyin', I better be the one who should watch my back.

Powers nodded and walked away.

Bronson stepped out of the room, whipped out his cell, and punched in the appropriate numbers.

Michael Hoover at the other end of the line picked up the phone on the fifth ring. "Homicide. Hoover."

"Hey, Hoover."

"Hey, Bronson. I've been talking to Paul McKenzie. Frankly, I'm beginning to worry about you. Don't you think it's time you contacted the Safford police?"

"And tell them what? That someone slashed my tire? Yeah, they could get the culprit on vandalism—assumin' they could find this mysterious *S* person or whoever did it. Then there's the notes. They never threatened me. They've just shown me how incompetent I've been. Nothin' criminal in that."

"Just be careful, buddy. What can I do for you this time?"

"Damn. Seems every time I call is because I need a favor."

"So what's new? You were never one for chitchat."

Bronson cringed. He'd have to work on changing that. "A charter flight in Tucson picked up a passenger by the name of Trent Powers and brought him here to Safford so he could attend the conference."

"Trent Powers? Why does that name sound familiar?"

"He was one of the fraternity officers in the same fraternity house where Casey Secrist was murdered."

"That's where I heard the name before. And you said he's there at the convention?"

"Yep."

"What's he doing there?"

"He claims he won an all-paid expenses to the convention."

"I don't like this, Bronson. I don't like it one bit." He cleared his throat. "My brother-in-law is a detective in Tucson. I talked to him last night. He's up to his eyeballs in paperwork. I'm sure he'll welcome the opportunity to get out and do some real detective work. I'll see what he can find about that charter flight and who hired them, which is what I assume you want to know."

"You betcha."

"Okay. I'll get back to you, soon as I hear from Dave."

"Thanks, again."

"Don't mention it. I'm keeping tabs, remember?"

Bronson smiled. He knew there wasn't anything Hoover wouldn't do for him or vice versa. "Yeah, yeah. I'll just subtract it from the ones you owe me."

"Ouch."

"I'll wait to hear from you." Bronson disconnected and returned to the consultant's party, his mind reeling with unanswered questions.

Chapter 20

The bartender flashed Bronson a frustrated look. "Just coffee, you said?"

"Yep. Plenty of cream and at least three heapin' spoonfuls of sugar."

"Sir, this is a bar."

"That serves drinks. Make mine a coffee."

The bartender sighed. "Right away, sir." He turned and poured the coffee.

"I thought you said you were down to two and a half level spoonfuls of sugar."

Bronson didn't have to look over his shoulder. He recognized that voice. It belonged to the love of his life who at this moment was probably the same person shooting darts at him—poisoned ones, at that.

The best defense is a good offense, Bronson remembered from his high school chess tournament days. "What are you doin' here?" This was work, after all, and he had always made sure that work and his private life never mingled.

Carol put her hands on her hips and flashed him a warning look. "You'd know that, if you had been listening to me yesterday."

So much for an offensive attack. Best to shift gears—quickly. He looked at the pleasant-looking woman who stood beside Carol. He noticed her badge. She was not one of the people on his list. "I don't believe I've had the pleasure of meetin' you, ma'am."

Carol perked up. "This is Gay Toltl Kinman."

Bronson knew that from the badge.

Carol rolled her eyes and sighed in frustration. "You know, Gay Kinman."

That hadn't helped. Bronson mentally checked the names of every case he'd worked on.

Gay smiled and offered Bronson her hand. "There's no reason why you'd know me. We've never met. I'm Gay Kinman and I write—"

"Children's books," Bronson finished for her and shook her hand. He felt proud he recognized the name. He looked at Carol and she smiled and nodded.

Bronson had scored a point. Now he knew how the male peacock displaying all of his feathers felt. "Our grandkids love your Alison Leigh Powers Mysteries. Didn't I hear somewhere your work had been nominated for several awards?"

Gay beamed. "Very nice of you to remember that."

"So what's a nice author like you doin' in a conference like this?"

"It's a great place to sell books. These people are mystery lovers and readers, and I find it fascinating trying to solve a case."

"How many people here are writers?"

"I'd say at least half."

That created about two hundred and fifty possibilities. Too large a number to work with. "Any idea who wrote the script?"

"No, sorry. That's one thing we don't discuss. It's like cheating. But we'll find out on awards night."

The waiter cleared his throat and pointed to the steaming cup of coffee. Bronson accepted the drink and handed the bartender a five-dollar bill. "Keep the change." He sipped the coffee. Perfect. He leaned on the bar and looked at Gay. "Is this the first time you've attended this conference?" His gaze shifted from Gay to Carol, and he knew she knew he was working, but not as a consultant. He'd have a lot of explaining to do once he returned to the room.

"Oh no. This is at least my sixth or seventh conference."

"So you no longer get the advertisements."

Gay's forehead creased. "What advertisements? L'ee has been running this conference as long as I've been coming. She's strictly a word-of-mouth advertisement type of person. She feels flyers advertising something like this cheapens it."

"So there's no contest, either."

"Contest?"

"Yeah, like first-place winner gets an all-expense-paid vacation to the convention site."

"Oh goodness, no." She let out a small laugh. "You apparently don't know L'ee. She's a fine person, but very much a tightwad." She sipped her drink. "An all-expense-paid convention contest? No, never."

Bronson finished his coffee and turned toward the bartender. Another cup of that delicious coffee would hit the spot just right. He smiled at the bartender who cringed.

Carol grabbed her husband's arm. "You better not be asking for seconds—not unless it has only two level spoonfuls of sugar."

Women. Why must they always be so health conscious? "I was just going to set the cup down."

The bartender perked up.

Bronson looked at Gay. "So what progress have you made solvin' the conference's case?"

"None, but that's because I'm not a player. My publisher kept delaying the release date of my latest mystery. I thought it wasn't going to come out in time for the convention, so I didn't register. But as it turned out, the book did come out. So I'm just here to promote my book and to chat with my friends."

Bronson inwardly smiled at the golden opportunity that just dropped in his lap. "So you're free to find out who wrote the script?"

"Yes, I am, but why would I want to do that?"

Good question. Why indeed? "I'll let you in on a secret." He lowered his voice and both Gay and Carol leaned closer to him. "There's a question about copyright. I need to warn the author before he or she reveals himself or herself at the awards thing."

Gay gasped.

Carol's eyes narrowed as she studied her husband.

"Goodness. That's serious." Gay looked around the room as though trying to figure out who could have written it.

"Then you'll help me find the person who penned the script?"

"Yes, of course."

"But you must keep this under wraps."

Gay put her index and thumb fingers at the edge of her lips and moved them along her lips as though she was zipping them shut. "Mums the word." She finished her drink and set the glass down on the bar. "I'll get on it right away." She turned and walked away.

Before Carol could say anything, Bronson turned toward her. "Carol Bronson, what are you doin' here?"

"If you'd been listening—"

Bronson slapped his forehead with his open palm. He should have known better. "That's a cop-out. What are you doin' here? You know by now that I never want you gettin' involved in my work."

"Correct me if I'm wrong. This is a mystery conference, and you're the consultant. Nothing else is going on, right?"

Bronson rubbed his chin.

Carol frowned. "Oh, Harry Bronson. How can you get yourself involved in another case so soon?"

Darn that woman. How did she do that? How did she always manage to find out? "I didn't—" He stopped. There wasn't really much to say. He removed his glasses and chewed on the earpiece. "This one came chasin' me."

"Meaning?"

"Meanin' don't mingle with these people. I'm not sure who's who or what's what. Until I do, I want you safe in the camper or in the room."

"I'm a big girl. I can take care of myself."

"I know you can. Heaven help anyone who tries to kidnap you."

"Is that a compliment or an insult?"

"A compliment, sweetheart. A compliment. Now get out of here."

"When you get back to the room, you and I—we're talking."

Oh-oh. "You betcha." He leaned over, kissed her, and watched her walk away. He then retrieved the spiral notebook he kept in his pocket. Only one name remained unchecked from the list he had made when he looked at the applications.

He wondered why Norman Childes had not shown up.

Chapter 21

Norman Childes hesitated to call his friend. One thing about him, he had a violent temper. One small glitch in the plans would set him off. Norman wiped his face with the palm of his hand. Might as well get the call over with. He grabbed his wallet and keys and headed out.

He had spotted the pay phone in the motel's lobby, but even that one would be too risky to use. Better walk across the street and use the one at the gasoline station. That should be safe enough. He wished he could use his cell, but if the call ever got traced . . . No, better to stick with the public phone. He should have grabbed his bottle of Tums. The acid in his stomach had doubled since this ordeal began. It would all lead to murder, again.

Casey's death had been enough and done with a long time ago. But this . . .

Norman heard the squeaking of tires and a horn blaring. He felt the air sucked out of him as he watched in horror the eighteen-wheeler approach.

Heart thumping, Norman stepped back onto the sidewalk. What was he thinking, stepping off into a busy street and not looking? Maybe he had a death wish.

Probably did.

He didn't want to be involved with someone's death again. His muscles tightened and he literally felt sick. Maybe the gasoline station would have some antacid medicine.

He waited until the traffic cleared before crossing the street. Without hesitating, he went to the phone, took out his handkerchief, and covered his palm with it before picking up the receiver. You can never be too careful.

He dialed the number by memory. As instructed, no where did he have the number written down. That small detail would protect his friend and him.

A hesitant voice at the other end answered, "Yes?"

"It's me, S—" He froze. A slip like that could cost him his job or even his life. "It's Norman Childes."

"That was very clever."

"I'm sorry, for a minute there I slipped and used—"

"No excuses. The bottom line is you messed up."

Even though Norman knew his friend couldn't see him, he nodded. "I'm sorry."

"Sorry doesn't cut it. What do you have to report?"

"Trent Powers is here. He and Bronson have been talking."

"About?"

"Too risky. I couldn't let them see me, and there was no place to hide. They talked for about fifteen minutes."

"We can't chance it. You know that, don't you?"

Norman broke out into a sweat. He nodded.

"Don't you?" his friend repeated, this time with more emphasis.

"Yes." Norman's voice came out barely above a whisper.

"Trent has been a thorn in our side for quite some time. He's lived long enough. Get rid of him."

Norman felt all the air leave him. He had feared this would be his command.

"Norman? Don't disappoint me. I surely don't want to lose you, too."

The line went dead.

Why Casey Had to Die

Carol heard the knock on the door. She hesitated. She remembered what her husband had told her. "Trust no one." She looked through the peephole. No one was there.

People are always knocking on the wrong doors. It happens in every motel, Carol told herself. No need to panic.

A surge of anger nipped at Carol's nerves. How dare he. Bronson had taken a perfectly happy trip and ruined it for her. She had half a mind to go out and . . . and . . . and what?

Mingle?

That's what she'd do. If she couldn't beat him, she'd join him. Maybe she could get some snooping done. Learn the ins and outs of the convention. That should help her husband.

Trust no one.

Carol paused. Surely, if she went down to the lobby where hundreds of people had gathered, nothing would happen to her.

She grabbed her purse and walked out.

Four doors down from the Bronsons' room, the hallway took a turn to the left. From there, Sam leaned against the wall and watched Carol leave the room. *Just as I suspected. She's becoming suspicious. Otherwise, she would have answered the door. Bronson must have warned her. All that means is that I'll need to move more carefully and definitely faster.* Sam smirked at the irony behind the thought.

Sam retrieved the cell phone and called room service. "We need more towels immediately. My spouse is taking a shower and the maid this morning must have forgotten to replace the towels." Sam gave room service Bronson's room number and disconnected.

Less than three minutes later, the elevator door opened

and a maid, a very pregnant girl who was probably still in her teens, stepped out carrying an armful of towels.

Sam walked toward her, key in hand, and said, "I'll take those."

The maid handed the towels over and started to leave.

"Do me a favor," Sam said. "I have my hands full. Could you open the door for me?"

The maid looked at the locked door, bit her lip, and hesitated.

"Hurry. My better half is almost out of the shower and will be very upset if the towels are not there. Sometimes my spouse has a terrible temper and won't hesitate taking this directly to the manager."

Still the maid hesitated. Sam glared at her. The nervous teen retrieved her key and opened the door for Sam.

"Thank you," Sam said and stepped inside Bronson's room.

Chapter 22

By now, most of the guests who attended the "Meet Your Consultant" gathering had wandered off toward the lobby, and Bronson had grasped the chance to speak to Tom and Marie O'Day. As an added bonus, Katherine Shephard joined them. Bronson nodded a hello. "Glad you all could come," he said.

"Thanks for the invite, but I'm rather curious." Tom sloshed the liquid in his glass and looked down at it. "What was the purpose of this gathering?"

Bronson scratched his chin. "Must there be a purpose to everythin'? Can't a group of people gather for the joy of it?"

"Not in your case. You had an ulterior motive."

"Yeah?" Bronson could use a cup of coffee. He turned to the bartender who quickly walked away. "What makes you think so?"

"My husband has made a hobby of studying people." Marie first looked at Bronson, then at Tom. "He finds you fascinating."

"Is that so? Since this is confession time, I find the three of you fascinatin', too."

Tom turned to the bartender and asked him to refill his Coke. "Actually, Marie is quite right. I formed several hypotheses about you." He handed the bartender two dollars for his drink.

When Bronson didn't comment, Tom continued, "I'd bet

you're the kind of guy who loves California. The ocean. Disneyland. The movie stars."

Not quite his style, but Bronson figured that O'Day was definitely working up to something. He'd play along. "Reckon most everyone is fascinated with that."

"True. True." Tom sipped his drink. "You go much to California?"

Bronson did a mental check. California? Wasn't that the state the previous consultant lived in? "Probably not as much as you've been there."

Tom looked at Marie.

Marie looked down at her hands.

Bronson looked at Tom and Marie. He smiled.

They smiled.

Bronson made a mental note to tell Paul McKenzie to extend his search for the O'Days to include California.

"I'm from Texas," Katherine said. "Best state in the union."

Bronson looked outside the room and spotted Carol. He had assumed she had gone back to the room. Darn that woman! "Can't argue with you. Texas is a good state. Mighty big and good." He saw Carol chatting with some of the convention attendees. "If you'll excuse me for a minute, I see someone I have to talk to."

After talking with Bronson, a black cloud hovered over Trent Powers. Bronson had not written the skit as he had been told. Then, to top it all, although Bronson hadn't specifically said anything, Trent felt sure Bronson thought the contest had been rigged. That meant Sam had made sure both he and Bronson showed up. Trent understood why Sam would want Bronson there, but Trent couldn't imagine why Sam wanted him, too.

Whatever game Sam had set up for them, Trent wanted nothing to do with it. He'd have a drink, then pack his bags, and off he'd go, even if he had to pay his own way back. He headed for the bar and ordered a rum and Coke.

"I'd like to buy you a drink. Can I just pay for that one?"

Trent turned toward the source of the voice. He felt the air sucked out of him. "You! What are you doing here?" He looked at the badge. It read Norman Childes. A million questions popped into his mind. This man most certainly wasn't Norman Childes.

Norman smiled as he fingered the badge. "Norman is my roommate," he said as though he had read his mind. "He accidentally picked up my badge, and he's somewhere around here wearing my name. So until I find him, I'm wearing his."

Trent nodded and saw Bronson walking out of the room. He would be very interested in learning this new turn of events. Trent might even consider leveling with Bronson. If Bronson knew the truth, he'd be better prepared and more alert.

"So, can I buy you that drink?" Norman smiled.

"Sure, but I was just heading to the can. Meet you here in a few minutes."

"I'll be here."

"Swell." Trent headed toward the restroom sign. He slowly turned his head so he could see if "Norman" was watching him. Not only was he not watching him, he had turned so that his back faced Trent.

Trent pivoted and headed toward Bronson. As he walked past the detective he said, "Need to talk to you. Meet me at the bar in ten minutes."

Bronson barely nodded an acknowledgment and kept on walking.

Trent continued to head toward the bathroom. A few minutes later, he returned to the bar.

He found his drink waiting for him, but "Norman Childes" was gone. Trent scanned the room but didn't see him. Might as well. He really didn't want to talk to him.

Trent reached for his drink while he waited for Bronson to join him.

Chapter 23

Bronson joined the group of women who chatted with Carol. The only one Bronson recognized was the author, Gay Kinman. He nodded a "hi" and put his arm around Carol. "Ladies, would you mind if I claim my wife back?"

Murmurs of "no's" and "of course not's" rang out.

"Good. In that case, say good night to these ladies."

Carol smiled and leaned her head on her husband's shoulder. "Sounds like I have a heavy date." She moved her eyebrows up and down.

The ladies laughed.

"Talk to you all later," Carol said.

Not if I can help it. Bronson led her away from the group. "What are you thinkin'? Thought I told you these people were dangerous."

"Oh silly. Look at that bunch. They're not very threatening."

Bronson turned to look at the group of women. He had to agree. The bunch of gray-haired women certainly didn't look dangerous. But one thing he had learned in this business, you never know. "Still." He flashed her a warning look.

"Let me tell you why I wanted to talk to them. I thought maybe I could find something that could help you."

Pride flowed through Bronson's veins, but he kept his facial features straight so as not to reveal his emotions. Last thing he needed to do was encourage her.

They reached the elevators and Bronson pressed the button. "So did you?"

"Not that I know of, but of course, I wouldn't know if I did or not because you haven't leveled with me, now, have you?"

Bronson closed his eyes and shook his head.

"Hey, at least I tried." Carol waited until her husband stepped inside the elevator. She pushed the button for the third floor. "I'm new at this detective thing. You're going to have to train me."

Bronson felt the blood leave his face. He probably looked whiter than the doughboy being dipped in flour. "Wh—wha—what . . ." Had he forgotten how to speak? He cleared his throat. "What did you say?"

Carol kissed his cheek. "Oh, you know the old adage. If you can't beat them, join them. I'm going to become your partner."

Oh, heaven forbid. Over my dead body. No, never. "We'll discuss it when I get back."

Carol's eyes popped open like two huge, brown buttons. "Where are you going?" She stepped out of the elevator and headed toward their room.

"I told Trent I'd meet him back at the bar. He apparently had something very important to tell me."

"Then I'll go with you." She turned back, heading toward the elevators.

"No!" Bronson grabbed her arm and led her back to their motel room. He wasted no time opening the door. "I promise that as soon as I get back, I'll level with you. In the meantime, I don't want to be worried about you. Promise me you'll stay here."

Carol pouted.

"You look so darn sexy when you do that. I have half a mind not to go back downstairs."

Carol brightened.

"But I don't have a choice." He kissed her and walked away. "Stay here." He closed the door behind him before Carol could protest. He prayed to God she would stay.

Chapter 24

As soon as the elevator doors opened, the shouts reached Bronson's ears. He stepped out of the elevator and noticed that a group of people had gathered to watch a shouting match. As he headed toward the commotion, he heard two ladies talking. "That's disgusting," one said to the other. "Two teenagers fighting and everyone gathers around them to watch. People are so disgusting. All they're doing is egging them on."

"You're so right. Downright disgusting."

They headed toward the elevators.

Bronson considered approaching the youths when he spotted the four hotel employees rushing toward the disturbance. Good, he wouldn't have to get involved unless it became absolutely necessary. Bronson heard the manager order the feuding teens to stop. "I've already called the police." His voice rang every bit as loud as the angry youths' voices had been.

"Shit," said one of them and ran out. The other teen hesitated for a second before dashing out. Bronson caught a fleeting glance of their backs.

The manager breathed heavily through his mouth. He formed a smile that looked more forced than friendly. "I'm sorry, ladies and gentlemen, that you had to witness this unfortunate scene in my peaceful inn. Please rest assured that nothing like this has ever happened before, nor will it—"

A piercing wail interrupted him.

Everyone's attention turned toward the source of the scream. One of the contestants, an elderly, white-haired lady, stood visibly shaking. Close to her, a body lay on the floor.

The manager and his employees froze. The crowd drew in their breaths, a mixture of fright, repulsion, and morbid fascination registered on their faces.

Bronson rushed to the victim's side. He felt his stomach tighten into a gripping, groaning knot as he took in the scene before him. Trent Powers lay dead by the bar, his spilled drink a puddle at his side. Had Bronson gotten here a minute earlier, he might have been able to save Trent.

Bronson pulled out a chair and helped the badly shaking lady sit. He then squatted and recognized the distinct odor of almonds. The foam in the victim's mouth confirmed Bronson's suspicion. Trent had been poisoned. Someone had slipped potassium cyanide into his drink.

Bronson stood and looked at the manager. "Did you really call the police?"

The slightly plump man stood with wide-open eyes. His complexion matched the color of a milk shake.

"Have you called the police?" Bronson repeated.

"Uh . . . I . . ." He shook his head.

"Call them now."

The manager nodded but continued to stare at the body. His hand flew up to cover his mouth.

Bronson turned to the hotel employee who stood next to the manager. Luckily, the assistant seemed to have better control of his emotions. "You." Bronson pointed at him. "Call nine-one-one and tell them to contact E.M.S."

"Right." He looked pleased that Bronson had chosen him to help. He started to turn, then stopped. "Nine-one-one and who else?"

"The Emergency Medical Service."

"Got you." He ran and the crowd made space for him.

Bronson raised his arms and gently waved them. The murmur died down. "Ladies and gentlemen, I realize this is a gruesome sight, and you'd rather go back to the safety of your rooms. I don't blame you, but I am goin' to ask you to do somethin' you won't like. I would like for each of you to stay here. The police will want to talk to you."

A waiter approached, carrying an empty round tray. He reached for the discarded glasses on the bar.

Bronson abruptly turned toward him. "Stop! Don't you dare touch anythin'."

"But it's just the empty glasses," the waiter protested.

Bronson pointed his forefinger at the waiter and growled, "Don't touch."

The waiter walked away.

Bronson pointed to the hotel staff who had gathered in a cluster and had anxiety written all over their faces. "Make sure no one leaves and that includes the hotel staff." He placed chairs in a wide arc around the body in order to protect the crime scene from possible contamination. "Did anyone see anyone leave?"

No one answered, not that Bronson had expected anyone to. They all had been too busy watching the fight. Whoever had done this had created the ideal distraction. "Can anyone here identify the two young boys who were fightin'?"

People looked at one another. Most shook their heads.

Bronson wished he had been able to see them, but by the time he had reached a visible position, all he saw was the blur of the youths' backs. He looked up to see if he could spot any security cameras. None existed.

Bummer.

Nothing left to do but wait.
The E.M.S. arrived within minutes.
Here we go, Bronson thought.

Chapter 25

Obviously, these conference attendees took their game seriously. Sheriff Ray Quaid figured that they either had to be serious TV detective show enthusiasts who eagerly absorbed police procedure much like a sponge, or they had actually had police training. Neither option appealed to him.

The county sheriff removed his hat and ran his fingers through his thinning hair. *Might as well get it over with.* "Who blocked off the crime scene?" Quaid looked at the crowd in the motel. They stared back at him like a herd of moose in pain.

One hand went up. What? Had someone failed to tell him they were back in school? Quaid sized up the man who had his hand raised. He was a solidly built man, perhaps in his early fifties or late forties. He had thick hair. Man, everybody had thick hair except him. Quaid approached him. "I'm the county sheriff, Ray Quaid. Thank you for securing the crime scene." He offered him his hand.

Bronson accepted it. "You're welcome."

The man has a firm shake, Quaid thought. This man is one tough cookie. "How did you know to do that, Mr. . . . ?"

"Bronson. Harry Bronson."

Bronson. Harry Bronson. Was that anything like Bond, James Bond? Quaid nodded and waited for Bronson to answer the other half of his question. When Bronson failed to say

126

anything, Quaid prompted him, "I assume you've had police training."

"You assume right."

Great, his fear had been affirmed. "Where?"

"Dallas, detective, retired." Bronson almost looked apologetic.

Which he should well be. Damn. Not only had he been a big-city cop, he had been a really big-city cop. Just his luck. Quaid hated big-city cops, and now he'd probably have to rely on him. "What's your connection to the victim, Mr. Bronson?" He felt sure Bronson carried a different title, but he'd be danged if he would use it.

Bronson's gaze focused on him like a laser beam. "We need to talk, but not here."

Great. Already telling him how to do his job. "If you have any useful information, you need to share it with me now."

Bronson didn't flinch. If nothing else, he straightened up. Stood taller. Fluffed himself up. "The victim's name is Trent Powers from Dallas."

Quaid's attention focused on the word *Dallas*. "So there is a connection between you and the victim."

"He was a witness in one of my previous cases."

"Tell me about this case."

"It's somewhat complicated. I'd rather we talk where it's a bit more private."

That man just can't help himself. There he goes, telling me how to do my job again. "Very well, as you wish." He signaled for one of the deputies to join them.

The deputy, a tall, thin black man, quickly approached.

Quaid pointed at Bronson. "Take him to headquarters, and make sure he waits there until I can get free from here."

Bronson said, "Carol—that's my wife—she's upstairs. I need to tell her what happened."

The sheriff felt a twinge of satisfaction when he heard Bronson's statement. "Sorry, Mr. Bronson, we need you at headquarters now. You've got a statement to give." He signaled for the officer to take Bronson away.

"Sir, you'll have to come with me," the deputy said.

Bronson quickly scanned the room and spotted his trusted friend, Gerri Balter. As he walked past her, he said, "Think you can notify Carol for me?"

"Of course." She smiled and gave him an encouraging nod.

Quaid waited until Bronson and the deputy had closed the door behind them before he resumed speaking. He turned to face the crowd. "Who's next?"

The crowd shrank back.

"Come on, folks, the sooner you talk to me, the sooner you can get on with your life. Who in here saw what happened?"

People looked away. Or down. Even at each other. Anywhere, but at him.

"Unbelievable. You expect me to believe that not a single one of you saw anything?"

"We were all focusing on the fight."

Quaid approached the young woman who had spoken. "You are?"

"Katherine Shephard, from the great state of Texas, but no relation whatsoever to Bronson. I'm just here attending the conference."

"Tell me about the fight."

"These two teens apparently are dating the same girl. They got into a shouting match. They almost started punching each other, but then the hotel manager and his buddies came in, threatening to call the police. The teens took off. Next thing we know, we hear this scream. We turn and . . ." She pointed to the crime scene.

"What did the teens look like?"

128

Why Casey Had to Die

"One had dirty blond hair and—"

"No. They were both brunettes," someone in the crowd chirped in.

Someone else said, "I could have sworn it was red hair. I remember admiring the fire-red hair."

"No, no, Louise. That was a red cap he was wearing."

"They weren't wearing caps."

"Weren't they bald?"

Quaid sucked in his breath. If he did that until he turned blue, maybe they'd all shut up. He inserted his thumb and middle finger in his mouth and let out a loud whistle.

Instantly, the din died. Some even stood at attention. "Does anybody feel he has something important to say?"

"I do."

Heads pivoted toward the source of the voice. Gay Toltl Kinman looked like a mouse in a cage filled with snakes.

Quaid approached her, and she took a step back. He opened his mouth to tell her that he didn't bite, but then he thought it might be better if everyone thought he did. "Speak."

"I'm not here to attend the—"

"Who are you?"

"I'm Gay Toltl Kinman and I write children's and young adult mystery novels. I'm here to mingle with my friends and this year I'm not participating in the conference. Bronson knew—"

The mention of Bronson's name triggered a set of warning bells in Quaid's system. "Bronson? The same Bronson who just left?"

"Yes, Detective Bronson."

So he was a detective. Great, great, great. Just peachy cream great. "What about Mr. Bronson?" He emphasized the word *mister*.

"He wanted me to find out who wrote the script for the

conference. He said there was a problem with the copyright issue, and he had to talk to the author before he or she revealed him or herself."

Reveal himself? What kind of a conference was this? "Back up. Give me details."

Gay explained how the conference ran and how everyone had to solve the crime that someone had scripted. "Normally, we don't find out who wrote the script until awards night which is the last night, but like I told you, because of this copyright technicality, Detective Bronson wanted me to find out who authored the script."

"Why are you telling me this? What's your point?" Quaid asked.

"Because I talked to every single person who enjoys writing and none of them claim to have written it. They all did tell me of a newcomer who likes to write."

"And that is?"

"The deceased. The victim. I strongly believe that he was the one who wrote the script."

Quaid raised his voice loud enough to carry throughout the room. "Did anyone in here write the script?"

Several shook their heads. Most remained quiet.

Quaid turned back to Gay. "Someone in authority has to know the answer."

Gay shook her head. "The manuscripts are sent via mail. The author doesn't put his or her name on the manuscript nor anywhere else. They are not even allowed to put a return address on the envelope."

Quaid slowly nodded. "So you think that the victim is the one who wrote the script and for that he was killed?"

"I didn't say that," Gay defended herself. "All I said was that he probably wrote it, and that Detective Bronson might know why someone would want to keep that a secret."

"Secret enough to be killed for?"

Gay nodded triumphantly.

Great. Everything led back to Mr. Bronson. Quaid wished he could interrogate Mr. Bronson immediately. He obviously could shed a lot of light on this case. Unfortunately, Mr. Bronson would have to wait until he finished talking to the folks at the motel.

Quaid wondered what kind of story Mr. Bronson would tell him.

Chapter 26

Quaid saw four deputies arrive. He signaled for them to join him. "I'm going to divide this crowd into groups. You're to get individual statements from each one of them. Do not interview any in front of the others. Take each of them aside and talk to him or her. I want to know if they saw anything. If they tell you something different from the rest, write that down. Get their name, address, phone number, E-mail if they have one. At the end, ask them if they feel there's anything we need to know." *Basic Crime Scene 101.* The deputies should be acquainted with that kind of information. Unfortunately three out of those four had only been on the force since yesterday. Quaid had no idea how much they knew or how they would react. Better baby them than be sorry later on. "Oh yeah, I forgot to tell you. There's some kind of a mystery they're supposed to be sorting out. Get details on that, too. Might as well cover all angles. Any questions?"

No one had any. Quaid divided the crowd into groups and assigned a deputy to each group. He was about to start interviewing some when he saw Louise Ligon walk through the door. She had remembered to bring the department's digital camera. Will miracles never cease?

If they were from Dallas like this Bronson guy, the department would have a fancy digital camera, one of those that did everything except take the picture without human assistance.

They also would have the money to train Louise on proper procedures.

But this wasn't Dallas, and he wasn't Bronson. He was a county sheriff and the camera wasn't the best technology had to offer, but at least they had a camera and a photographer. Quaid turned to Louise. "Get several pictures from each angle. Get some of the glass on the floor. Maybe even some room layout pictures."

She eagerly nodded and got to work.

"As of now, the bar is closed," Quaid said loud enough so everyone could hear him. He heard several moans and groans as a response. What? Did these people really think they'd still be able to buy drinks?

He waited until Louise had taken several pictures of the glass. He squatted and recognized the faint odor of almonds. Cause of death, poison. Self-inflicted or murder? Quaid made mental notes. He picked up the glass by its lip and dropped it in a plastic bag. He recorded all of the important information and tagged the bag.

A toxicology screen would confirm his suspicions and a fingerprint analysis would hopefully reveal the culprit. Case closed. How's that, coming from a county sheriff, eh, Bronson?

Quaid approached the bartender who stood with his arms crossed absorbing all the commotion around him. "You're the bartender on duty?"

The youth opened his mouth to speak. Nothing came out. He nodded.

"What can you tell me?"

"N . . . not . . . much. I . . . I swear. I didn't do nothing. The dude asked for this drink."

"What kind of drink?"

The bartender shrugged. "Normal drink. Rum and Coke.

I fixed it just like I did all the others. Nothing special. Just rum and Coke."

"And you served others from the same container?"

"Before and after."

"Anybody sit with him, talk to him?"

"Yeah, for a while I saw him and some other dude talking."

"Can you describe this 'dude'?"

"Yeah, he was big."

"How big?"

"You know, big. Muscular. Not fat. Trim, for a guy his age."

"How old?"

"Oh, dunno. Not old, old. Just old. Why don't you ask him?"

"Who do I ask?"

"That guy who was talking to the dead guy. I remember him because he kept asking for coffee. You know who I mean. He started to give you all of this lip, so you finally sent him to jail, I guess."

The edge of Quaid's nerves stood at attention. "You mean Bronson?"

"Yeah, that's him."

Bronson. Bronson, again.

Damn!

Sam's stomach tightened into a hard knot. If Sam could look in a mirror, it would most likely reveal a ghostly complexion. But that was all right. Everyone around Sam looked and felt the same way.

No one would notice anything different, but one hell of a difference existed. Trent lay dead, the victim of a poisoned drink. All according to plan. The only glitch was that Sam hadn't done it. Yet someone had, just according to the plan. A plan no one other than Sam knew existed.

Chapter 27

Bronson considered asking the youthful-looking black deputy for a cup of coffee. But as amazing as he found it, the idea did not appeal to him. Right now, coffee would agitate his already jittery nerves.

Now he knew how those guys he left sitting in the interrogation room felt, but dang it, he wouldn't give them the satisfaction of seeing him squirm. He slumped in the chair, interlocked his fingers in front of his chest, and closed his eyes.

He figured he must have slept because when he opened his eyes again, almost two hours had passed. He scanned the room. No Sheriff Quaid. How much longer, he wondered.

He looked around the small, crowded room. Not much to keep him entertained. He stood up and his nervous escort panicked. "Uh, sir . . ."

Bronson looked at him, smiled, and headed toward the door.

"Sir, uh, you can't . . ."

Just as Bronson reached for the doorknob, his cell went off. He looked at the caller I.D. Michael Hoover. Bronson turned to the deputy. "Do you mind? I have to take this call."

The deputy shifted positions. He looked at the closed door and back at Bronson. "No, of course not." He stood in front of the door, crossed his arms and leaned against the wall.

Bronson rolled his eyes. So much for privacy. He flipped the phone open. "Hey, Hoover."

"Hey, Bronson."

"Don't tell me you've got the information this fast."

"Okay, I won't tell you that, but I do have the information. Like I told you, Dave was just itching to get out of the office. He went to the airport. From the flight plan, he found the name of the charter. Logan's Air Taxi. Dave talked to the pilot and the owner, which luckily for him turned out to be the same person, is a guy by the name of Eddie Logan. Turns out Logan remembers Trent quite well. Logan said that some guy who claimed to be Trent's brother walked into his office."

"Trent's brother?" Bronson didn't know Trent had a brother.

"Yeah, his brother. He tells Logan that Trent is arriving on a Southwest plane, Flight 608 from Dallas. He asked Logan to pick him up and take him to Safford. He paid cash and other than a receipt, there's no paperwork on the brother."

"What about a description? Can Logan identify him?"

"No, not really. Logan said he was—and I'm quoting—'an ordinary-looking man. He's not too tall or too short.' Couldn't remember the color of hair or eyes. Far as he knew, there were no distinguishing marks. Dave couldn't get anything else out of him."

"Give me the brother's name and contact information and I'll follow up."

"As usual, I'm one step ahead of you. I checked the brother out. Trent is an only child."

Bronson closed his eyes and rubbed the bridge of his nose. Another dead end. "Thanks to you and your brother-in-law for all the work both of you did."

"I'm sorry it didn't work out. Dave said he was going to spend some time in the airport. He'll talk to the employees and see if any of them remembers anything. If something develops, I'll call you."

"I appreciate that."

"Stay safe."

"I am. In fact, I'm in the sheriff's office. How much safer can I be?"

"Good. I see you decided to take my advice after all."

"Not quite. Seems like someone poisoned Trent Powers. I think the sheriff thinks I had something to do with that."

"You're kidding, right?"

"Wish I were."

"Do you need for me to go down there?"

"Nah, buddy. Nothing you can do." He saw the front door open and Quaid stepped in. He looked tired and angry. Not good for either of them. "I'll call you later. The sheriff is here."

"Be careful."

"Always." He closed the phone and returned it to his pocket. He looked up as Quaid entered his office.

He signaled for Bronson to follow him. "You're next."

Bronson felt he should salute him and come to attention. "Yes, sir."

Quaid flashed him a whimsical look. He led him to a metal desk Bronson assumed belonged to Quaid. He pointed to a chair. "Sit down. Care for a cup of coffee?"

"No, thanks. It's past my bedtime. It'll keep me up." Bronson heard himself utter those words. Amazing. He thought he'd never say them.

"Suit yourself."

Bronson sat in front of the desk, facing Quaid. Once Bronson sat down, the young deputy departed.

Quaid waited until he was out of hearing range before he turned his attention to Bronson. "Tell me what you know."

Here we go. Bronson took a deep breath. "First case I ever worked on—"

Quaid slapped the desk with the palm of his hand. "Are you trying to be funny? Let's begin at the beginning of the current case."

"I am, but it has its beginnings in my first case."

Quaid slowly nodded. "Yeah? This is going to be interesting." He leaned forward. "Tell me about your first case."

"A young college girl got killed while attending a fraternity party. At first it looked like a simple overdose, but eventually her boyfriend was indicted for her murder. He slipped her some liquid ecstasy. Seems that he wanted to pacify her so that she'd offer little or no physical resistance to having sex. However, I've always felt that we sent the wrong person to prison."

Quaid remained quiet, then it dawned on him. "Damn! Isn't that the same case that mystery group is supposed to be solving?"

"Right."

"And you say the boyfriend didn't do it?"

"That's my feelin'."

"Have you talked to him?"

"A week after he was incarcerated, he was conveniently killed in a prison accident."

Quaid frowned. "You think someone caused this accident to happen?"

"Just maybe."

"You said this was your first case."

"That's correct."

"Then you've had a lot of time to research it. What have you come up with?"

"Not much. Early in the case, I was pulled out. Told the case had been solved. Drop it, forget it, don't ever mention it."

"And you did."

"The opposite. Eventually it forced me to retire. Seems I had a problem followin' policy."

"And now that you're retired?"

"Now I can work on it in an unofficial capacity. Records have always been closed so it won't be too different workin' on it now."

"So you created this little skit to open up the case."

"Sorry to disappoint you, but I did not write that skit."

"If not you, then who?"

"There's one person who knew about the case. He was, in fact, one of the fraternity officers. Same fraternity that hosted the party where Casey died."

"And that is?"

"Trent Powers."

"The deceased."

"Yes. Prior to his death, he told me that he was there because he won some kind of a contest. I never had a real chance to follow up on that, but the little that I did showed it to be bogus. But apparently he received an all-paid conference. He arrived in Tucson on a Southwest flight. The tickets were mailed to him. Once in Tucson, he flew out on a charter flight, Logan's Air Taxi. Supposedly Trent's brother made all the arrangements. It turns out Trent has no brothers or sisters. Contact information on that is Dave—sorry, I don't have the last name—a detective in Tucson. You can also contact Detective Michael Hoover in Dallas. He can hook you up to Dave." Bronson wrote down Hoover's office phone number and handed Quaid the paper.

Quaid glanced at the paper and put it under the phone. He

drummed the table with his fingers. "You figure Trent wrote the skit?"

Bronson shrugged. "I confronted him about it. He denied writing it."

"So what do you make of that?"

"He knew somethin'. That's for sure. He made it a point to walk toward me. As our paths crossed, he very discreetly asked me to meet him in the bar in ten minutes."

"What did he have to say?"

"Nothin'. He was killed before he could tell me whatever he had to say."

"How convenient." Quaid bit his lower lip as he thoughtfully looked at Bronson. "Any witnesses that can confirm your story?"

A warning bell rang inside Bronson. "None that I know of. Like I said, he didn't want anybody to know he wanted to talk."

"So it's all on your say so."

Bronson nodded. "Get to the point, sheriff."

"Do you realize, Mr. Bronson, that in the skit, there's a detective assigned to the case?"

Bronson once again nodded. He was getting real good at that. "I am familiar with the skit."

"I assume each character in the skit has its real-life counterpart."

"That's correct."

Quaid thumbed through his notes. "The detective in the skit is Fred Reid. Tell me who Fred Reid is supposed to represent in real life?"

For a while Bronson remained quiet. Somewhere along the conversation Quaid had switched from being his supporter to being his adversary. He wondered how much he should tell him.

"Didn't you hear my question, Mr. Bronson? Who is Fred Reid's equivalent?"

"That'd be me."

"A hotshot detective. Brand new to the division. He's got to prove to everyone on the force he can solve each case. Would that sum you up pretty well?"

"Hotshot? Not really. Never cared for the limelight. Eager? Yeah, maybe so. What are you drivin' at?"

"You may be interested, Mr. Bronson, in some of the attendees' findings. Several have found that the girl did indeed overdose. Drugs killed her, but she willingly took them. Now here comes this hotshot detective. He's assigned to his first case which turns into a no-case. So what does hotshot detective do? He creates a case. You know, plant a little evidence here, a little there. He solves the case. Instant hotshot status. What do you think?"

"I think you didn't think this through. If Hotshot Detective framed Poor Boyfriend, why would Hotshot Detective be trying to prove him innocent after so many years? Seems to me Hotshot Detective would want to keep the case closed."

Quaid pointed at Bronson. "You know, you may have a point."

Great, Bronson thought. Just as I get him maybe convinced that I'm not the bad guy, then I hit him with a double whammy. "There's something else," Bronson said. "Better hear it from me than from anyone else."

"Yeah? What's that?"

"There's a rumor going around the conference that I caused Max Iles' accident."

"Who's Max Iles and what accident did you cause?"

"I didn't cause any accident and I have no idea why the rumor got started. But Max was the previous consultant."

"Was? Like he's dead?"

"Max was the victim of a fatal hit-and-run accident. His death, of course, vacated his position, and I was offered the job."

"Who offered you the job?"

"Wayne Weeks, Events Coordinator at the Lodge."

"And how did he get your name?"

"He was looking for someone to fill the position. He glanced down and saw the Dallas newspaper, opened to the article about me."

"A Dallas newspaper? Where did he get a Dallas paper?"

"Weeks explained that the Lodge is a motel. People carry newspapers from all over the country. They read them. They leave them behind."

"Logical, but also highly coincidental. Tell me, Mr. Bronson, how do you feel about coincidences?"

Never believed in them. "Once in a while, they could pop up."

"Yeah? You really think so? I don't, so let me give you a word of advice. You better watch your back and your front, 'cuz I'm going to be watching every step you take."

Great. Just what I need. The good guys and the bad guys are now both after me.

Chapter 28

Bronson stepped out of the back office room and into the entryway. Carol stood up and hugged her husband. He kissed her forehead. "How long have you been here?"

"Came over just as soon as Gerri told me what happened. Been here for over two hours." She looked at her watch. "Almost three. What's going on?"

"They just had some questions, that's all."

"They told me they weren't holding you. Were they?"

Bronson wrapped his arm around her and led her out. "Technically, no, but I couldn't just walk out, either."

"You have some explaining to do."

"Let's get a cup of coffee and I'll fill you in."

"Must it be coffee?"

"I've earned it."

Carol sat silently through her husband's narration. When he finished, he emptied his cup and stared at Carol. At this moment he wouldn't blame her if she clobbered him.

Carol took in a deep breath. "Oh, Harry Bronson, what am I going to do with you?"

"Forgive me and love me?"

"That I can do. This time you really are innocent. You didn't go looking for a case. It's just like you said. It came looking for you."

Bronson felt the air being sucked out of him. "But?"

143

"But nothing. We've had this conversation before. I know for sure now that I'm joining forces with you. I'll mingle. See what information I can get."

"You'll do no such thing."

"Try and stop me, Harry Bronson."

"Aeyee." Bronson hit his forehead with the palm of his hand.

Bronson had spent the last two hours reading over his notes. He made charts, added notations, drew diagrams, floor plans, and studied the results some more.

His first priority involved providing Carol with a number of harmless activities that seemed to be important, yet remained relatively safe. For this, he'd call Gerri who in turn would call other people whom she knew would be safe. Together, they could go out "investigating." There was safety in numbers. Bronson liked that.

Next thing on his agenda involved paying Dolly Secrist another visit. He picked up the phone to let her know he was coming.

As soon as Dolly swung the door open, the aroma of a freshly baked apple pie tickled Bronson's nostrils. "Evenin', ma'am."

Dolly smiled and stepped aside so Bronson could step in. "Detective Bronson, it's always so good to see you."

"Pleasure is all mine." He sniffed the air like a hound following a scent. "Might that be apple pie?"

"Freshly baked." She wiggled her eyebrows. "I even got some coffee brewing for you."

Now, here's a woman who knows how to please her guests. Aloud he said, "Lead the way, then."

Dolly laughed and the wrinkles around her eyes formed,

giving her the look of a gentle, warm person. "Follow me."
She led him to the kitchen.

Sammy Kiewell sat at the kitchen table, a half-full glass of
milk in front of him and a half-eaten chocolate chip cookie.
He looked at Bronson and squinted. "Are you here to eat my
cookies again?"

"Sammy!" Dolly scolded.

Bronson laughed. "You remembered. You're a bright,
young boy."

Sammy beamed. "Okay, you can have some." He offered
Bronson the cookie he had been eating.

"Very kind. But today I'm here to eat some apple pie."

Sammy shrugged and stuffed the rest of the cookie in his
mouth. "Cookies are better." He finished his milk and set the
glass down. "Can I go play, Grandma?"

Dolly nodded and pointed to his wooden wagon. "Why
don't you walk around the house and see how many toys you
can pick up from the floor and put in your wagon?"

"One toy for one cookie?"

Dolly smiled, bent down, and kissed his forehead. "I'll
add it to the number of cookies I owe you."

"Okay." Sammy pulled his wagon behind him as he
walked out of the kitchen.

"Cute kid," Bronson said.

"Adorable. Just absolutely adorable." She set two slices of
pie à la mode on the table and poured Bronson his coffee.
"But as much as I delight in talking about him, I'm sure
you're not here to talk about Sammy."

Bronson took the time to put the sugar and milk into his
coffee. He stirred it before answering. "I'm here about the job."

Dolly pierced a small piece of pie and with slow, deliberate
moves, stuffed it in her mouth. Anyone watching her would
have assumed she had to judge its flavor. "Job?"

"You know, I was hired to be the conference's consultant." He sipped his coffee, but not once did he remove his attention from Dolly's gaze.

"Oh, that job." She wiped her lips with a cloth napkin. "What about it?"

"I want to know how I was hired."

"Goodness, didn't you tell me that Wayne Weeks hired you?"

"I did."

Dolly attempted to smile, but it came out looking more like trembling lips. "Then?"

"I'd like to know how Wayne Weeks found out about me."

"Didn't you tell me that he read about you in the Dallas paper?"

No, I didn't. "And you subscribe to this Dallas paper?" She had already told him she did, but he wanted to verify the information. He watched her lips tighten and her nostrils flare.

"No . . . yes." She looked down at her slice of pie as though it would vanish if she looked away. "I know what you're thinking." Her voice came out as a whisper as though ready to reveal some sinister plot. "You think I gave him the paper. Suggested your name."

"I think you left the paper lyin' around, opened to that page. Weeks saw it, and knowin' that you're from Dallas, asked you about me. I'm sure you gave me a very good recommendation."

"Nothing wrong with that."

"No, nothin' at all, but I want to know what you thought you'd accomplish by havin' me here."

Dolly gave a small shrug. "Thought I could get you to look at Casey's case all over again."

"And how were you goin' to do that?"

"I . . . I don't know. I didn't think ahead."

Bronson reached out and wrapped his hands around Dolly's. "Tell me what you're not tellin' me."

Dolly let her breath out as though she'd been punched in the stomach. She withdrew her hands and looked down. "I . . . I don't know what . . . you're . . . talking about."

"Oh, Dolly. Dolly. Dolly." Bronson finished his pie and pushed the plate away. "Best apple pie in the country. It's as good as it smells."

Dolly's lips twitched as she gave him a small nod.

Bronson leaned back on his seat and folded his hands over his chest. "Tell me about the newspaper."

Bronson heard a noise coming from somewhere in the living room. Sammy with his toys. Bronson heard the clock tick, the television play. Outside, a car zoomed by. A dog barked.

He wished he had more coffee but didn't want to break the momentum he had built. He focused his gaze on Dolly.

Slowly, she looked up and when she saw him staring at her, she quickly looked away. "What did you say?" she asked, her voice small and timid.

"The newspaper."

"Oh, yes, the newspaper." She sighed and looked around the room. Her gaze rested on each object as though she were seeing it for the first time. "I cancelled my subscription to the Dallas paper a long time ago."

"I figured as much."

Dolly looked at him, squinted, and shook her head. "You're amazing, you know that?"

"Am I now?"

"You knew all along and you never let on. What else do you know?"

"You tell me."

Dolly took in a deep breath and sat up straighter. "I received the article in the mail one day. In the same envelope I also received some information about the conference and a little typed note saying that Wayne would be hiring a consultant. I thought maybe once you were here, I could convince you to work on Casey's case. Then I got to thinking. Someone sent me that article about you retiring and about the position opening. I figured whoever did could easily be connected to Casey's case. Why else would I receive those clippings? Wayne and I are sort of seeing each other—" She flashed Bronson a quick glance. There was a twinkle in her eye and a blush in her cheeks. "Anyway, I put the article down in a place I knew he'd find it and, as they say, the rest is history."

"You didn't by any chance keep the conference information you received or the envelope it came in?"

Dolly gasped. "No. I should have. I didn't think." She closed her eyes. "I'm so sorry."

"What about a return address?"

Dolly shook her head, then brightened. "But I did look at the postmark. It was mailed from here, Safford."

Not much help. Whoever had mailed it had made sure he didn't reveal his real hometown. Bronson made a mental note to add this detail to his list of loose ends. "Tell me, Dolly, how much trouble did you go to to get me here?"

"No trouble. No trouble at all. Once Wayne saw the article and I told him what a good detective you are, he brightened. He was really worried about finding the right person."

"And once I got here, how did you plan to get me involved in Casey's case?"

"I figured you knew I was here. You'd come see me. We'd talk about Casey. I'm even willing to pay you to look into the case."

"That's not necessary. I made you a promise a long time

ago to look for Casey's real killer, no matter where I was, how old I got. I aim to keep that promise."

Dolly closed her eyes. "I know. It's just that sometimes I get so depressed. You'd think that after twenty years . . ."

"Since you received that article and flyer, has anybody contacted you about the case?"

Dolly shook her head.

"Do you know anything about the conference, how it's run?"

Again, Dolly shook her head.

"I believe you." Bronson stood up. "This much I'll tell you. Your wish came true. I'm workin' on Casey's case."

Dolly gave him a genuine Crest smile. "Thank you, Detective Bronson. Thank you."

"You're welcome. All I'll ask of you is to never keep anythin' from me again. Promise?"

Dolly stood up. "Promise."

"One more question. Do you know who wrote the manuscript?"

"What manuscript?"

"For the play—the mystery the conference attendees are supposed to solve."

"No, I didn't even know there was a manuscript."

Bronson could tell she spoke the truth. He wished she had written it as an attempt to get him involved, but things were never that simple.

And he knew things would only get worse.

Chapter 29

A nap is a nap, no matter where the napper naps, Quaid thought as he glanced at the couch in his office. Often, he or one of his deputies slept there, mostly on weekends or holidays when the place filled up with drunks, and the area needed more officers on duty. Every once in a while, Deputy Quintana slept there and everybody knew he'd had another fight with the little missus.

Quaid headed toward the couch once more and felt the house keys in his pants pocket calling him. Nah, the couch at work wouldn't do. The one at home, that's a different story. There, he could slip off his shoes, loosen his pants, and stretch out on the couch while his family was out of the house. He would catch up with the much-needed sleep he had missed out on because of this Bronson thing.

As he drove home, he felt the lullabies of sleep lure him, but of course, he resisted. After all, he reasoned, everyone expected the sheriff to stay awake, at least during working hours, and more often than not, during non-working hours, too.

He reached home just in time to hear the phone jingle. He sprinted toward it and picked it up on the fourth ring. "Sheriff Quaid." He heard an audible sigh and realized he had made a mistake. He shouldn't have identified himself. He pressed the phone closer to his ear, straining to hear whatever he could.

A brief silence passed, followed by a soft voice, one level above a forced whisper. "Sheriff, you don't know me, but I'm one of the conference attendees. Thought maybe you'd want to know. Day before Trent died, I heard Bronson and his wife talking. She mentioned something about a vial, and he immediately hushed her. Way they talked made me think there was something sinister. Then Trent died—well, I thought maybe you'd want to check Bronson's room, or at least know about the vial."

A loud click followed and Quaid knew the informer had disconnected.

Quaid replaced the handset in its cradle and his hand lingered on the phone. The informer had called his home phone, probably thinking he wouldn't be talking to him directly.

Early in his career, Quaid had chosen an unlisted number. Very few people had this information. Yet someone had called him, someone with connections enough to get his home phone, and chances were that connection led back to Bronson.

Quaid wondered if Judge Kile would give him a search warrant based on an unidentified informer's call. Maybe Quaid would have to rely on friendship, and maybe ask for a favor. He hated that.

Out of the three towns that shared the valley, Safford, Thatcher, and Pima, Safford reigned as the largest, but even so, by anyone's stretch of imagination, Safford could not be considered a large town.

Consequently, Bronson reasoned as he waited for the light to turn green at the intersection between Staghorn Avenue and U.S. Highway 191, finding the two teens who had probably been paid to stage the fight should not be too difficult. A couple of trips to the high schools, some properly asked questions, and perhaps the clincher, a reward offered, would lead to the actors.

Only problem with that, Quaid would probably arrest him for interfering with an ongoing investigation. Times like these, Bronson missed officially being called detective.

The light turned green and Bronson turned onto Highway 191, heading back toward the Lodge. Maybe if he called Quaid and offered to follow up on the quarreling youths—

The ringing of his cell disrupted his thoughts. He recognized the ring as belonging to his lab buddy, Paul McKenzie. Bronson pulled over and answered the phone. No need to give the sheriff a reason for ticketing him for driving and talking. "Hey, Paul."

"Hey, yourself. Got your mystery solved."

"That's what I like to hear."

"That's why I called."

"Okay. Now that we got that straight, how about gettin' to the mystery?"

"Spoil sport."

"That's me." Bronson scanned the area. No cars had pulled off when he did, and none had turned on the next available corner. Seems like Quaid hadn't requested a tail. Surprise, surprise.

"Hoover tells me you've been held for Trent Powers' murder. Are they crazy over there or what?"

Bronson smiled. It was nice knowing he could always rely on Hoover and Paul for moral support—or any other kind of support, for that matter. "You know how ornery I am. They couldn't hold me. No evidence, but I'm still their number-one suspect." He looked around. Still no sign of a tail. "So what mystery did you solve?"

"The O'Days. Remember I told you they didn't seem to exist?"

"I remember." Bronson continued to watch the street behind him.

"That's because the O'Days name is an alias. Their real names are Victor and Betty Lowes."

Even though Bronson knew that Paul couldn't see him, he nodded. He had assumed that O'Day was an alias, but now he knew for sure. "How did you figure that out?"

"Those glasses you sent with the fingerprints. They matched the Lowes'. I then got on the computer and googled them."

"And what did you learn about the Lowes?" Still no trace of a tail. Either these guys were very good or he wasn't being followed. Bronson suspected the latter.

"Nothing you want to hear. They've got clean records, not even an outstanding parking ticket. They live and work out of San Bernardino, California."

San Bernardino? Wasn't that where the previous consultant, Max Iles lived? "What else can you tell me about them?"

"He's a private investigator."

Interesting.

Chapter 30

Although the Lodge's parking lot had been designed to accommodate more cars than the Lodge had rooms, it was filled to capacity. Murder obviously was good for business. Bronson drove through the parking lot twice before he found a parking space. Naturally, it had to be on the opposite end from his room.

He headed for the side door and inserted the room card in the slot. The door opened and Bronson stepped into a side hallway, thus avoiding most of the crowd. He headed directly for the elevator and punched in his floor number.

Just as the elevator door closed, it reopened and Katherine Shephard stepped in. She flashed Bronson a courteous smile.

"Ms. Katherine, ma'am. Are you, like the O'Days, from California?"

"Yes." Her eyes snapped open. "No. Like I told you before, I'm a Texas girl." She quickly punched in her floor and the door closed. She focused her attention on the closed door.

"Maybe you're a Texas gal at heart, but you reside in California. Tell me, did you know Max Iles?"

The door to the elevator opened and Katherine bolted out. "Later, Detective Bronson."

As Katherine stepped out, Gerri stepped in. "There you are." She reached to punch her number. "Oh shoot, this is going up. I wanted to go down."

"Eventually this will go down. In the meantime, you have the distinct honor of ridin' with me."

Gerri threw her head back and laughed. "That, I do." Turning serious, she added, "You missed the meeting today."

"What meeting?"

"L'ee called a meeting. Due to the circumstances, we voted to disband. Some of the conference attendees have already checked out. Most, of course, are staying. I mean how often do we get a chance to participate in a real, live murder mystery?"

Bet Quaid loved that, Bronson thought, then wondered if L'ee would still pay for his motel room now that he no longer worked as a consultant.

A third thought hit him, and he blurted out, "What about the script? Do we know who penned it?"

Gerri's eyebrows arched. "No, I'm sorry. L'ee didn't mention it. I should have brought it up. But maybe she didn't say anything because she knows who wrote it." She shrugged. "Maybe."

The elevator door to Bronson's floor opened. He stepped out. "Let's hope so. Thanks for tellin' me about the meetin'."

As the doors closed, Bronson saw Gerri wave good-bye. Bronson smiled and headed for his room.

Carol had just stepped out of the shower and was in the process of drying off.

Bronson walked over to her and his lips brushed hers. "Looks like I arrived just at the right time," he leered and moved his eyebrows up and down in fast succession.

"You bet—but not for the reason you think. You're in time to take your shower and take me out to dinner."

Bronson kissed her lips once more. "We're not eating

downstairs?" He'd been looking forward to a quiet evening with Carol. Maybe even ordering room service.

"Nope, too crowded. Ever since poor Trent's death, this place is abuzzing. Besides, the gals told me about this super Mexican food restaurant in Solomon called La Paloma."

Visions of hours spent driving to the restaurant filled Bronson's mind. "Where?"

"Solomon. It's a tiny town, not too far from here."

"Define 'not too far.' "

Carol rolled her eyes. "You're such a baby. Fifteen-minute drive, maybe? Twenty, tops. Anyway, listening to everyone rave about La Paloma makes the drive worth the time. People come from all over just to eat there. I've got directions and I'll be driving us."

Bronson brightened. Was there such a thing as Mexican coffee? He'd soon find out, and he wouldn't have to bother with the driving. Not bad. "I'll take a two-second shower and be ready to go in ten minutes, tops." He winked.

She rolled her eyes and walked away.

He took off his shirt as he headed toward the bathroom.

Once Bronson stepped out of the shower, dried, and got dressed, Carol approached him. He looked at her, ready to tell her he'd be able to walk out within three minutes. Instead, he stared at her, concern nipping at his nerves. The frown she wore created deep crease lines in her forehead and around her eyes. Her breathing came at strained intervals.

Bronson wrapped her in his arms. "What's wrong?" He could almost hear her heart beat at a fast pace.

"Someone's been in our motel room."

The maid? Had she taken something? Could Carol have simply lost it? "What do you mean?"

"I opened the middle dresser drawer, the one where I keep my underwear. You know I always check the drawers to see that they're clean, empty."

"Yeah?"

"Someone went through my underwear and put this inside those navy-blue panties I have." She raised her closed hand and handed Bronson something. She let the item fall on his opened hand.

Bronson looked at the closed vial. He opened it and smelled it. The distinct odor of almonds reached his nostrils. "Shiiiiit!"

"What? What is it? Is it something bad?"

"Yeah, I'd say so. Most likely, this is the vial that contained the poison that killed Trent."

Carol's eyebrows arched as she pinched her lips together, making her look like a comical cartoon character. "Oh my God. What does that mean?"

It means that the vial now contained both of their fingerprints. "We need to call Quaid."

Carol gasped. "You don't think . . . he'll think, you . . . we . . ."

"Yes, he will and that's exactly what the perpetrator wants him to think. I'm quite certain you weren't meant to find the vial, and I bet you anything Quaid has received an anonymous call. He's probably right now in the process of gettin' a search warrant."

"We could drive out to the desert and bury it."

"Carol, that would be destroyin' evidence." His voice came out harsher than he had intended. He hugged her and stroked her hair. "We're going to do the right thing."

"But you told me Quaid already thinks you're guilty. This will only add to that." Her eyes beamed with tears.

"Maybe not. This might have been the killer's biggest mistake. Someone is bound to have let the killer in. We'll be able to trace him that way."

Bronson reached for the phone and dialed the sheriff's number.

Chapter 31

"You wanted to play detective. Here's your chance," Bronson told Carol. She sat at the edge of the bed, her back ramrod straight, her complexion matching the white bed sheets.

Bronson sat beside her, placed his hand on her leg, and rubbed it. "You okay?"

She barely nodded a response.

"You sure?"

She sighed and shook herself as though attempting to shake away the problem. "I'm a detective. Tell me what you need done."

"I want you to go over every bit of space. Check under the bed and under the mattress. Check inside every drawer and make sure nothin' is taped to the top or bottom of the drawers. Check the medicine cabinet and our suitcases. In general, check every area you can think of and those you didn't."

"What am I looking for?"

"Anything that doesn't belong to us."

"And if I find something?"

"Don't touch it. Show it to Quaid."

"You're leaving." A statement, not a question. Resignation in her voice.

"I'm not going far. Just downstairs. I'm going to go see if I can talk to all of the maids who clean this room. Hopefully,

one of them will know somethin' or have seen somethin'."
Bronson stood up. "You sure you'll be okay? Would you
rather I stay with you?"

She reached for her blouse and fixed it. "Don't be silly.
We detectives are strong and tough. You go do your thing,
and I'll do mine." She flashed him a smile filled with both determination and strength.

Bronson hugged his wife and kissed her. "You're worth
more to me than all the gold in the world."

"That doesn't mean much. Now, if you had said than all of
the coffee in the world . . ."

"Don't push it."

She stuck her tongue out at him. He tried to grab it. Both
giggled and Bronson walked out.

The manager's office seemed unusually small, perhaps because of the excessive amount of furniture cramped into the
room. A large wooden desk with four leather chairs domi-
nated the area. Four file cabinets, a bookcase, and a small
table with six fold-down metal chairs completed the let's-
have-the-office-appear-to-be-cramped look.

"I don't really understand, Detective Bronson, do you
want to file a complaint?" The manager, a short man with a
receding hairline and thick glasses peered at Bronson.

"Not exactly. All I want is to talk to the maids who clean
my room. Maybe one of them saw someone lurking outside
the room. Or maybe even while they were cleanin', someone
came in. I don't want to cause any waves. I just want to talk to
them."

The manager frowned. "I just don't see how you can talk
to them without filing an official complaint." He opened
his side drawer and thumbed through his folders. He pulled
out a paper and shoved it toward Bronson. "You fill that

out. I'll go see who was on duty."

Bureaucracy, Bronson thought. He hated it. He reached for the form and started filling it out.

As soon as Lupe received the call to report to the manager's office, she knew she was in trouble. Somehow no matter where she went, what she did, bad things always happened to her. Well, not anymore. If she kept quiet, if she didn't reveal anything, everything would be all right. She hadn't, after all, done anything wrong.

Now more than ever, she needed this job. Jobs weren't too plentiful in a small town like Safford, especially if you were Catholic instead of Mormon. Maybe if she had stayed in school, she could have . . .

Don't go there. She forced herself to stop thinking along those lines. She didn't have, after all, a single regret. No, sir. Not a one. In less than a month her little one would be born. Then she wouldn't be lonely anymore. Not ever.

She stroked her tummy and looked at her reflection in the mirror. Her normal brown skin looked so pale. Maybe it was the pregnancy. Maybe it was the fear of losing this job. Maybe it was both.

"I promise you, little one, I will keep the job. I won't be fired. I'll be a good mommy. I'll provide for you."

Lupe stepped out, determined to play the I-don't-know-anything role. She was good at that.

It startled Lupe to see Vicky already there. Both of them cleaned the same rooms along the same hallways. She eyed the stranger sitting in Mr. Lamont's office. He was tall and powerful looking. Probably rich, too. What did he know about working as a maid? All he wanted was to create problems for a poor, hard-working girl like her.

"Ladies, this is Detective Harry Bronson from the Dallas Police Department."

The police! Lupe hated policemen. Trouble always surrounded them. Now, more than ever, she realized she had been right. Mums the word.

Bronson looked at both her and Vicky and Lupe felt as though the detective scrutinized her soul. Did he know about her past? Did it somehow show? She focused on the floor. She spotted two places that needed to be cleaned.

Bronson placed his hands behind him and paced as he spoke. "Ladies, thank you for comin'. Me and the little missus, we're stayin' in 304. You ladies know that room?"

"That's our floor. Me and Lupe clean it. Something wrong with the service?" Vicky stood proud and tall. Her voice boomed with courage. Lupe envied her.

"No, none at all. I think you ladies are doing an outstandin' job. Place couldn't be kept better."

The gentleness in his words, the soft, kind voice startled Lupe. What kind of policeman was this? She looked up at him and found he had stopped pacing and stared at her. She immediately looked down at the floor.

"Thank you, sir." Vicky's tone sounded more relaxed. "So what's the matter?"

"I'd like for you ladies to think back. Was there ever a time maybe while you were busy cleanin' the bathroom that someone came into my room? Perhaps you heard a noise. Saw someone. Naturally you'd think this person belonged in this room. It's only natural."

Vicky's eyebrows shot up in the air. Her eyes opened as wide as saucers. "Someone broke into your room? Stole something?" The look of fear replaced the initial shock. "Wait a minute. It wasn't me." She looked at Lupe. "Us. We clean. We're honest people. We find money on the floor, we put it back on the dresser."

"That's very commendable of you both. Not many people would do that." Bronson walked over to Lamont and patted his shoulder. "In fact, your boss here had already told me what hard workers both of you are and one-hundred-percent honest."

Vicky sighed and gave out a small smile. "Then. . . ."

"Bottom line: someone came into my room. There's never been any sign of a break-in. Someone either has a key or someone let them in, willingly or unwillingly."

"Not us." Vicky stepped closer to Lupe. "We always put the cart in front of the opened door. No way someone can come in without us hearing. It's as much for our protection as for the customers'."

"That's very impressive. I hope that's a policy all cleanin' engineers follow."

"Everyone at this hotel does." Vicky's face beamed with pride.

"That is commendable." Bronson once again placed his hands behind him and resumed his pace. "You're awfully quiet. Do you have anythin' to add?" Without looking up, Lupe knew the policeman was talking to her. Yes, she had something to say. She remembered the customer demanding the towels. Lupe had brought them up and opened the door. What a fool. She had assumed . . . How could she know? Would she be fired now? "It's as Vicky says. We're careful to place the cart so that it blocks entry to the room." Did her voice really sound squeaky? Could he hear her heart beat ever so loudly?

Seconds dragged and Bronson remained quiet. Lupe could feel his gaze focusing on her. He knew. Best to say something. It had been an honest mistake. She opened her mouth to speak but Lamont spoke up, interrupting whatever she might have said.

"I suppose that clears you both." He looked at Bronson. "I'm sorry they couldn't help."

Bronson frowned as he looked away from Lupe to Lamont. "Thank you, ladies, for comin'." He handed each a card. "I wrote down my room number and my cell. If either of you remembers somethin' or sees someone unusual by my room . . ."

Vicky grabbed the card. "We'll call you."

Bronson turned to Lupe. "Ma'am?"

She reached for the card and wished her hand wouldn't shake so badly.

Bronson smiled. "Talk to me. I'm not the enemy."

Lupe almost felt like smiling back. For a policeman, he sure was nice. She'd have to think about what she should do. It could all be a trap. Better to keep quiet.

Vicky and Lupe turned and walked out.

There were several things Bronson wanted to do before heading back to the room. But by now Quaid had probably arrived and it wasn't fair to leave Carol by herself. He quickly headed for the elevators.

While waiting for it to open, he saw Tom sitting on a couch, reading a newspaper. Bronson glanced at the numbers indicating the floor the elevator was on. The elevator was stuck on the sixth floor. He had enough time to at least get a reaction from Tom.

Bronson considered walking up to him and calling him by his real name just to see how he'd react. As Bronson approached him, he realized that might involve more time than he had to give. Instead he said, "Hey, Tom."

Tom looked at Bronson and set the newspaper down. He nodded a hello.

"Ever heard of Solomon?" Bronson asked.

"Solomon? Like in the Bible?"

Bronson smiled. "No, the town. Supposed to be maybe a twenty-minute drive from here. My little missus and I are going there to eat in a restaurant called La Paloma. Supposed to be real good Mexican food. I know you want to talk to me, and heaven knows, I want to talk to you, too. We'll be there in maybe an hour or so."

"I'm sure Marie and I can find the place. You said in about an hour?"

"Or so."

Tom nodded. "We'll talk then." He picked up the newspaper and continued reading.

Bronson walked away.

Chapter 32

Mighty coincidental. That's what Quaid would call it.

First he gets a call about searching for a vial in Bronson's room. Then Bronson calls, reporting finding the item. Too easy. Too convenient.

Quaid hated it when that happened. Didn't believe things fell in place like that. Sure as weeds spring, something was brewing. What that happened to be, Quaid couldn't be sure but he'd bet his reputation, Bronson had to be at the root of it all.

The sheriff pulled into the Lodge's parking lot, parked the car, took a deep breath, and stepped out. *Here goes nothing.*

He wondered what kind of a story Bronson and his wife—what was her name?—concocted. He knocked on the door and waited. And waited some more. What the—

The door slowly opened just far enough for a lady to peer out.

He flashed his badge. "You must be Bronson's wife."

She nodded.

"I'm the sheriff. Quaid's the name and your husband called me."

She nodded once again, closed the door, unbolted it, and reopened the door. "Come in, Sheriff. My husband will be back any minute."

"He's not here?" Why did that not surprise him?

"He went downstairs to talk to the maids who clean this

166

room. He thought maybe they'd seen somebody lurking in the hallway or maybe even in our room."

Quaid shook his head. "Ever the detective, is he?"

"It's in his blood. I don't think we'll ever be able to separate the two."

Wonder why that makes her sad, Quaid thought. "Tell me about the great find."

"Not much to tell. I took a shower, opened the drawer to get my . . . huh, clothes, and there it was."

"On top of your clothes."

"No, actually buried at the very bottom of everything."

"Then how did you happen to find it?"

"The item I wanted was toward the bottom and when I pulled it out, the vial came rolling out."

Another coincidence. Quaid retrieved his notebook and jotted down the main ideas.

"My husband does that, too."

Quaid looked up from his note taking. "What?"

"Takes notes on a little notebook he keeps in his pocket."

Great. I always wanted to be just like Bronson. He closed the notebook and returned it to his shirt pocket along with the pen. "Then what happened?"

"Harry was in the shower."

"Who?"

"Harry, my husband. Bronson."

He knew that. He just wanted her to verify it. "Go on."

"After he got out, I gave it to Harry. He opened it, smelled it, and immediately said we were calling you."

The door opened and Bronson stepped in. "Sheriff Quaid."

"Bronson."

"Hope you haven't been waitin' too long."

"Just got here. In fact, your wife was telling me what happened. Let me hear it from you."

167

"I stepped out of the shower. Carol comes in. She was visibly shakin' and hands me the vial. Said she found it in the drawer and was sure it wasn't there before."

"How would she know that?"

"My wife is very meticulous. She always checks the drawers to make sure they're clean and that no one's left anythin' there. If my wife says the item wasn't there before, I simply believe her. It wasn't there."

Quaid nodded. "I see." He turned to Carol. "Can you show me exactly where you found the vial?"

Carol turned bright red. "I . . . I don't think so."

"And why not?"

Bronson wrapped his arm around his wife. "Because she found it in her underwear drawer." He turned to Carol. "Sweetheart, I realize this is embarrasin' for you. After all, this is your personal stuff. But for us policemen—" He looked at Quaid. "—law enforcers—whatevers—they're just clothes and nothin' more. Why don't you show him where you found it?"

Carol frowned and headed toward the bureau. "Second drawer to your right." She pointed to the drawer.

Quaid opened the drawer, and Carol, brighter than Snow White's shiny apple, looked away. "Can you show me exactly what happened?"

Carol looked at Bronson with pleading eyes. He nodded an encouragement. She frowned. "I reached for my . . . huh . . . undergarments—like I told you, the one I wanted was towards the bottom. When I pulled it out, the vial rolled out. I didn't know what it was, so I picked it up and looked at it. I set it on the dresser while Harry showered. When he stepped out, I handed it to him."

Quaid shook his head. "You handed it to him. So now it's got both of your fingerprints. How very convenient for you,

Detective." He stretched out the word *detective,* making it sound like an insult.

Bronson made sure he maintained a poker face. "I could have simply taken it out to the desert, buried it, and it would have never been found—or if it had, no one would have recognized it for what it was. Instead, we did the right thing and called you."

"Very thoughtful of you." Quaid closed the drawer. "I suppose if I were to search the rest of the room, I'd come up empty-handed."

"You're welcome to search, of course, but while Harry was downstairs, I checked the room from top to bottom. I looked in all of the usual places as well as those unusual places, like under the drawers, between the mattress and bed frame—stuff like that. I didn't find anything," Carol said, "other than a lot of dust bunnies." She dusted herself off, as though remembering all of the hidden dirt.

"Of course you didn't find anything out of the ordinary. And if I were to search myself, I know I'd also come up empty-handed."

"What exactly do you mean by that?" Carol's harsh tone seemed to reprimand him.

Bronson placed his hand on his wife's arm and shook his head.

That didn't stop Quaid from responding. "It means that Bronson—the world-famous detective—knows exactly what to do and what not to do." Quaid switched his attention from Carol to Bronson. "I'll play your game, but only to a certain point. You better make sure neither of you disappears."

The sheriff headed toward the dresser. "I assume this is the vial." He pointed to the item resting by Carol's rings.

"It is," Bronson said between clenched teeth.

Quaid retrieved a small plastic bag and without touching

it, placed the vial in it. "If by some chance, I find some fingerprints that aren't yours or Carol's, I'll let you know." He sealed the bag and stuffed it in his pants pocket. "For the sake of convenience, would you mind if I take your fingerprints?"

"Anythin', in the spirit of cooperation," Bronson said. *Asshole.*

Chapter 33

After Quaid walked out, Carol flopped down on the bed. Bronson sat beside her and wrapped his arm around her. She leaned her head on his shoulder. He stared at the bureau, a plain, off-white, painted piece of furniture. How could such an insignificant piece of furniture cause so much trouble?

Without raising her head off his shoulder, Carol asked, "Now what?"

"Now I'm goin' to talk to the people at the front desk to see if you or I requested to have our room card re-keyed."

A frown crossed Carol's forehead. "We've never . . ."

"Exactly."

Carol slowly nodded.

Bronson continued, "I also plan to talk to security, see if they noticed anyone unusual or if someone reported anything of interest. Afterwards, I'll find Lupe and talk to her."

"Who?"

"The maid. I'm sure she knows somethin'."

"What about me? Is there anything I can do?" Carol asked.

"Sure. I want you to drive us to La Paloma in Solomon."

Carol turned to gape at him. "You're willing to take time off to eat?"

"I'm willing to take time off to be with you."

She smiled. "Retirement becomes you."

"You become me. I hope you always know that." He

kissed her. "On the way over, I'll tell you about maybe eating with the O'Days."

Carol placed her hands on her hips. "Oooohhh, Harry Bronson!"

"What? What did I say now?"

The drive to Solomon proved to be a relaxing time through the country roads. Most of the scenery consisted of farmland and wide-open spaces. From the outside, the restaurant itself reminded Bronson more of someone's medium-size home rather than a fancy eating place.

Once inside, they went down the wide hallway that led to the somewhat small dining area. Soon as they stepped in, Bronson spotted the O'Days. "Well, I'll be. Just whom I wanted to talk to," Bronson said.

Carol poked him in the ribs. "How did you manage to do that?"

"What can I say? I've got magic. Since they're here, and I need to talk to them, would you mind if we all sit together?"

"Sure, why not? Why would I ever think we could have a nice, peaceful meal, just the two of us."

"We can do that. We'll talk to the O'Days, then move to our own table."

"That would be rude. It's okay. We can eat with the O'Days."

"You're sure now?"

"I'm sure. Besides, maybe I'll get a couple of pointers on how to be a detective."

"That's the spirit." Bronson reached for his wife's hand and led her to the O'Days' table.

Tom looked up from the menu. "Bronson." He nodded at Carol.

"Mind if we join you?" Bronson asked, pulling out a chair for Carol. He sat next to her.

Tom's forehead furrowed. "I thought that's why you invited us to have dinner with you and your wife."

Underneath the table, Carol kicked Bronson. He flashed her a mischievous look and shrugged. "On my way back from talkin' to the maids, I might have bumped into Tom and mentioned we were eatin' here. Glad you could join us."

She kicked him again.

Bronson moved his legs to the other side of the chair. Looking up at the O'Days, Bronson said, "This is my little missus, Carol, the best wife in the world. Carol, these are the O'Days, Tom and Marie. They're from California."

A look of surprise flashed in Tom's eyes, but as quickly as it came, it vanished. "Nice to meet you. Anyone married to this man deserves a medal."

"I couldn't agree more." She looked at Bronson and pulled her face.

Okay, maybe I deserved that. He rubbed the tip of her nose and smiled. God, he did love this woman. She put up with so much B.S. from him. "Anyone know what's good in here?"

"I assume it's the first time for all of us, but the gals at the convention told me that just about everything here is good," Carol answered.

They got down to the serious business of studying the menus. The waitress came, took their order—Bronson felt a bit disappointed that there was no such thing as Mexican coffee—and brought them their drinks. Bronson picked up his coffee mug and raised it, offering a toast. "To our first conference. May next year's be a lot better."

Bronson clicked his mug to everyone's glass and drank.

"Prior to this terrible thing that happened, were you both enjoyin' the conference?" Bronson asked the O'Days.

"You bet," Marie said. "Good as always."

Bronson feigned surprise. "Oh really? Why had I assumed this was your first?"

Marie shrugged and looked at her husband. He set the chip he was getting ready to eat down and glared at Bronson. "I've been studying you," Tom said.

"Have you now?"

"Yes, and I know you know what I mean." Tom ate the chip. "See, that's the main difference between you and me."

"And what might that be?"

"I have something to say, I come straight out and say it. You? You casually mention something vague, then wait for the person to reveal something incriminating."

"Nothin' wrong with that."

"Other than making people feel completely exasperated, I see nothing wrong with that."

"Me neither." Bronson reached for a chip, dipped it in the sauce, and ate it.

"You're doing it now."

"Doin' what?"

Tom sighed and looked away. "You obviously have a reason for wanting to talk to us."

"Obviously."

Tom waited for Bronson to explain himself, but when he didn't, Tom continued, "I want to know what you know about us."

Bronson took in a deep breath while considering how much he should reveal. The O'Days would probably prove to be trustworthy people, but he still decided to feed them a little at a time. Better safe than sorry, he thought. "I know this is your first conference."

"And how do you know that?"

"Folks—they like to talk. They say, 'Tom and Marie

O'Day have never attended a conference before.' " Their food arrived and they waited until the waitress finished with her task.

Once she left, Tom looked at Bronson and said, "Okay, what exactly does that mean?"

"Just what I said. Nothin' more. This is yours and Marie's first conference."

"And if I tell you you're wrong? We have attended before."

Bronson opened his taco and looked inside. He scooped out a small piece of shredded beef and ate it. "Mmm, good." He closed his taco. "Then I'd say that maybe Victor and Betty Lowes have attended, but definitely not Tom and Marie."

Marie's eyes opened wide and her eyebrows arched. She looked at her husband. "He knows. How—"

Tom's stern look silenced her. He stared at Bronson.

Bronson bit into his taco and leaned toward Carol. "Thank your friends for suggestin' this place. Really good."

"I can do that," Carol said.

"We took a lot of pains to keep our identities hidden," Tom said. "I'd like to know how you found out."

"Fingerprints don't lie."

This time it was Tom's turn to wear the surprised look. "You had us fingerprinted? How?"

"Fair's fair. I've been answering your questions. Now's your turn to answer some of mine."

Tom frowned and slowly nodded. "I'm a private investigator. We're undercover."

Bronson wiped his mouth. "Lowes and Lowes Private Agency."

"I should have known you'd know that, too."

"Which means you still haven't answered any of my questions."

"Go ahead and ask, but before you do, I really want to know how you got my fingerprints."

"We got latent prints from a glass you used. When we checked the database, we found that you've been arrested. Why's that?"

Tom smiled and with a wave of the hand dismissed its importance. "I was arrested for Sneaking and Peeking. One of my customers hired me to check on his cheating wife. One night, I was snooping around the house. She apparently saw me and called the police. Once the police realized who I was and what I was doing, they dropped the charges."

"But you never had your fingerprints expunged?"

Tom stared at Bronson with a blank look. "No, I didn't."

"Well, that's why we found your prints."

"I'll need to remember to have that done."

"You do that."

Tom nodded. "So what's your question?"

"Why the charade?"

"I'm surprised you didn't find that out."

"Could have, but I decided to go to the source. So much more efficient that way."

Tom half laughed, half smirked. "I suppose so." He finished his enchiladas and pushed his plate away. "Okay, I'll come clean with you." He sipped his soda. "We were hired to investigate you. L'ee was a bit concerned that Weeks hired you over the other applicants who had been on the waiting list for so long. Max's death seemed a bit too convenient to her, and she hired us to make sure you weren't involved."

"But outside of L'ee and Katherine Shephard, no one knows about your true identity."

"That's correct."

"And Katherine is . . ."

"My cousin, just like we told you. Katherine Shephard is

her real name and she really is a Texas gal although she's been living in California for the past three years. She helps us at the office and does a pretty good job at whatever we ask her to do."

Bronson nodded. That would explain why she pushed so hard about him killing Max. She was hoping to trap him. "She did good. Didn't work, though, simply because I'm innocent."

"We realize that." Tom reached for his glass and emptied it. "Tell me, Detective Bronson, aren't you curious to find out what else we know about you?"

"You've found that I was a detective in the Dallas Police Department, that I'm an honest man, that I don't follow policy, and that's why I was given the option to retire early."

Tom nodded. "Did I find anything else about you?"

"Yep, you've found out I had nothin' to do with Max's death and that I can be a pain-in-the-neck when I want to be and sometimes even when I don't want to be."

"That just about sums up what I've learned. Maybe I could have saved myself a lot of time if I had just come straight out and asked you."

"Live and learn."

"There is one more thing I learned about you."

"And that is?"

"That you always have ulterior motives for doing what you do. Like dinner tonight. Did you invite us so you could probe our minds as to what we know?"

"Basically, and I've accomplished that."

"But there's more."

Bronson leaned back in his chair and took a deep breath. "Someone is tryin' to frame me." He told them about the vial and how at the convention, the mystery the attendees were supposed to solve was a real case, his first case.

Tom's interest increased with Bronson's narrative. The more details Bronson revealed, the more Tom leaned forward to hear him better. When Bronson finished speaking, Tom looked at him and rubbed his forehead. "Wow. I had no idea. You, my friend, got yourself in a real doozie."

"That's a very accurate diagnosis." He looked around the room for the waitress. When they made eye contact, he pointed to his empty coffee cup. "I need your help."

"What would you like us to do?"

"Stay undercover. Snoop around. See what you can dig up."

"I can help, too," Carol offered. Everyone's attention turned toward her. "I'm having lunch with L'ee tomorrow at Brick's." She focused her eyes on her husband as though daring him to stop her.

Bronson felt as though his breath had been taken away. "When did this happen?" He forced his voice to come out smooth and calm.

"I've told you. I've been doing my own snooping. Who better to talk to than to L'ee herself? And if I approach her, she won't suspect that we know anything."

Bronson frowned. Carol could be so logical at times. It irritated him. "I'm not sure I want you—"

"We're a team now. Just like Tom and Marie. Just like Victor and Betty."

One way or the other, he was going to have to get used to the idea of having a new partner. Dang that woman. "Very well. You work on L'ee, the O'Days will follow their own leads, and I'll do my own thing." Whatever that may be. "One way or the other, we'll get this thing resolved."

Chapter 34

Carol and Bronson enjoyed a room-service breakfast in their room while they watched the morning news. When they finished eating, Carol said, "I only have two chapters left in the book I'm reading. I'm going to go to the pool, do a couple of laps, and finish the book." She grabbed her swimming suit and headed for the bathroom.

Good, Bronson thought. She'll be busy and I won't have to worry about her. He stuck his head in the bathroom. "I'm going to go check with security while you're in the pool."

Carol nodded and Bronson rushed out.

The head of security was a feisty, eager individual with a hooked nose, similar to an eagle's. He shook his head with such determination that it drew attention to his nose. Not an eagle's nose, Bronson decided. A witch's nose. "No, sir, we definitely haven't seen anyone suspicious and no one has reported any break-ins. Not in my motel, not ever. Sorry you think otherwise."

Bronson had expected as much. "Thank you for checkin'. If you—"

"Find or hear anything, we'll let you know, but don't count on it. I run a very tight ship. Anything goes down, I immediately know about it. Criminals know that. They just stay away from here."

If only it were that simple, Bronson thought. He nodded,

stood up, and headed for the front desk. "Someone broke into my room," Bronson began.

The youth behind the desk gasped and reached for the phone.

"No, wait. Let me finish." Bronson raised his hand, encouraging him not to panic. "The sheriff has already been here and the motel security knows about it. I'm just doing some follow-up research. I'm Detective Harry Bronson from the police department. What I need to know is if anyone asked any of you to re-key their card, but instead of giving you their room number, they gave you mine. I'm in room three-o-four."

The youth shook his head. "Sorry, sir, I couldn't tell you if we keyed any cards to your room. I don't remember doing any, and I'll ask the other desk clerks. Besides, whenever we key a card, we always ask for identification. So if the card to your room was keyed, you or your wife or whoever you're sharing the room with had to be the one requesting the service."

Bronson nodded. "I thought as much." He started to turn, then decided against it. "One more thing. I'd like to talk to Lupe, the lady who cleans our room. Where could I find her?"

The desk clerk looked at some papers and back up at Bronson.

"I'm Detective Bronson and this is an official police matter." He was glad the clerk hadn't asked him for his badge and hoped he wouldn't do so now.

The youth's eyes widened, reached for the papers, and looked through them until he found the information he was looking for. "She's not scheduled to come in until one. She's often late. She'll be cleaning the rooms on your floor."

"Thank you. You've been very kind." He turned to leave.

"Detective?"

Bronson turned around.

"Sorry about your room."

Bronson flashed him a smile but knew the real reason he had called him back. He wanted to make sure he answered to the word *detective*. That was good. Showed the youth was thinking even though he hadn't asked for his badge.

Bronson looked at his watch. It was almost eleven. He didn't like leaving Carol alone for so long. Bronson hurried back to the room.

As he stepped inside, Carol was about to step out. "Whoa, where are you off to?"

She turned back, set her purse down on the dresser, leaned against it, crossed her arms and said, "I'm meeting L'ee, Gay, and Gerri for lunch, remember? We're the four musketeers."

He remembered. He had hoped she'd forgotten. "So where are you eatin'?"

"Brick's! The gals always rave about it, and now I'm going to get to try it. L'ee says they have the best beef tips."

"Sounds like you'll have a good lunch." He sat on the bed.

"I think so. What about you?"

Bronson patted his stomach. "Can't eat like I used to when I was younger. I might just skip lunch."

"Are you sure?"

"I do it all the time, but I'll be expectin' to have dinner with my lovely wife."

She leaned over and kissed him. "It's a date." She grabbed her purse and walked out.

Bronson stared at the closed door, forcing himself not to run after her. What was the matter with him, anyway? Carol has gone out to eat with "the girls" a million times before, but not with these girls. Well, so what? Neither Gerri, L'ee, nor Gay seemed to pose a threat—which was his point. Looks were often deceptive.

L. C. Hayden

Stop that! Get busy doing something productive. Maybe if he read his notes one more time, something would pop up. He read through them, again and again. Same-ol', same-ol' stuff. *Casey Secrist, daughter of Dolly Secrist. Lived at home until she went off to college. Moved in with her older cousin, Eleanor Jorgeson. Eleanor: a bit on the wild side. Introduced Casey to Alpha Kappa Lambda fraternity brothers.*

Frat house: Donald Stockwell, president; Ken Chalmers (now TX senator), vice-president; Trent Powers, in charge of pledges.

Harmon Moises: desperate to pledge; somewhat of a nerd. Stockwell, Chalmers, and Powers do not consider him pledge material. Moises was Casey's date to pledge party. Moises is charged with giving Casey date-rape drug, pleads innocent but is convicted. He's found guilty. He claims innocence. Sent to prison. Killed in prison riot less than a week after arrival.

Bronson set the paper down and rubbed the bridge of his nose. What was it that eluded him? Good detectives went by their gut, and right now, it told him the answer lay buried in the notes.

He again re-read them, not that he needed to. He had them memorized. He looked at each sentence individually, then at each word. He considered the different relationships.

Nothing.

After twenty-odd years, still nothing. Yet he knew it had to be there. His gut never lied to him—or maybe it was just telling him to feed it. Suddenly the idea of lunch appealed to him. Maybe he should try Brick's. Nah, that wouldn't be fair to Carol. Instead, he'd order a sandwich and a good cup of coffee. The prospect refreshed him.

Afterwards, he'd talk to Dolly one more time. Maybe together they could find that piece that would complete the puzzle.

★ ★ ★ ★ ★

Soon as Carol stepped out of the elevators, she saw the door to L'ee's room standing open. Carol approached but did not enter. She stood in the entryway and called out, "L'ee?"

"Yes, Carol, come in," came L'ee's chirpy voice.

Carol stepped in and noticed that the room looked identical to hers. Same plain wooden furniture with the same hanging light fixtures. Carol nodded at Balthasar who stood next to L'ee.

He grinned a hello.

His rugged looks disarmed Carol. *If only he'd grow some hair, he wouldn't look so tough and scary.* Composing herself, Carol turned to L'ee. "I'm looking forward to Brick's," she said.

L'ee grabbed her purse. "Good. In that case, let's go."

Carol looked around the room, hoping to spot her friends. "What about Gay and Gerri? Aren't we going to wait for them?"

"Gerri has somewhere to go after lunch, so she's taking her car. Gay decided to ride with her so she won't have to drive alone. They'll meet us at the restaurant."

"In that case, I'm ready to go."

"Me, too." With Balthasar's help, L'ee stood up. They headed out and Carol followed them.

Once they stepped out of the elevators, Balthasar said, "I'll get the car and meet you ladies out front." With that, he increased his pace and left them behind.

By the time Carol and L'ee reached the front door, Balthasar had driven the car to the front door and had opened both passenger doors. Balthasar helped L'ee in and closed the door. He checked Carol's door, stepped in the driver's side, and drove off. As he pulled out of the parking lot, he turned left.

Carol wondered why he had done that. She could have sworn that the restaurant was to their right. Heading the wrong direction did not seem to bother L'ee any, so Carol chose not to mention it.

Chapter 35

Once Bronson reached the hotel's restaurant, he changed his mind. He really wasn't hungry, and eating just for the sake of eating was certainly not good. That meant he'd get to Dolly's one full hour earlier than what he'd told her. He whipped out his cell phone and cleared it with her.

"In that case, I'll get the coffee brewing," Dolly said.

That made Bronson's taste buds stand at attention. If he were lucky, maybe she had made a new batch of chocolate chip cookies. He'd like that. He reached into his pocket for the car keys and spotted Gay typing on her laptop. What was she doing here in the motel? Bronson approached her. "Hi. Workin' on your next book?"

Gay looked up from her work and smiled. "No, actually just checking on my E-mails. I hate for them to pile up."

"I see." Bronson looked around the room. "Are you waitin' for Gerri?"

Gay's forehead furrowed. "No. Why should I be waiting for her?"

Hadn't Carol mentioned Gay, Gerri, L'ee, and she were going to lunch? Maybe he had just thought she said Gay. He really should pay closer attention. "Sorry. My mistake. I'll be seein' you around."

"Sure enough." Gay turned her attention back to her work.

Bronson walked away and headed toward the car, an uneasy feeling brewing deep within him.

★ ★ ★ ★ ★

He made it to Dolly's street in record time. He wasn't sure if that was because his mind had been working on the problem at hand, and that made the time go faster. No matter. Trying to focus hadn't worked. His thoughts returned to the image but the gray, fuzzy areas prevented him from seeing the entire frame.

Bronson cleared his mind and concentrated on his surroundings. Almost directly in front of him, Mt. Graham towered above him some ten thousand seven hundred feet. The San Carlos and White Mountain Apaches considered the land sacred, and no wonder. The pines and the oaks, the streams and lakes, all provided awe-inspiring views, or so Bronson had read. One of these days, before leaving the area, Bronson would definitely have to take Carol and drive up its scenic roads.

Bronson smiled. Recalling what he had read about Mt. Graham had led him back to thinking about Carol. Amazing. He pulled into Dolly's driveway. Maybe now he'd get Carol out of his thoughts. He rang the doorbell.

Sammy opened the door. "You're not a stranger. Grandma said not to talk to strangers. What does Stranger look like? Do you know him?"

Behind him, Dolly came rushing. "Enough, Sammy. I've told you before, a stranger is someone you don't know."

By the time Dolly finished with her explanation, Sammy had bounced off somewhere deep into the house. Dolly unlocked the screen door and Bronson stepped in. "Evenin', ma'am." He immediately recognized the scent of brewing coffee.

"Hi, Bronson. Good to see you, and before you ask, yes, the coffee's ready."

"That's my gal." He followed her to the kitchen where

Dolly poured Bronson the coffee and handed it to him. He looked around but didn't see any cookies. Bummer.

He stirred in sugar and cream. His gaze wandered toward the embroidered napkins with the *S* initial. *It's been a while since I've heard from S.* He wondered if that was a good or a bad thing. He looked up at Dolly and found her studying him.

"I've known you long enough to know that something is bothering you," she said. "What's wrong?"

Bronson took a large gulp of coffee and set the cup down. "As always, so very good."

Dolly smiled and nodded once.

"I'm here hopin' you'll help me grasp that vital piece of information I'm missin'."

"I'll be glad to help, but I'm not quite sure what you want."

"I want you to tell me about Casey."

The agonized look that came over Dolly's face told Bronson that the years had not erased her pain. She glanced away and covered her face. Slowly, she moved her hands away and turned her attention to Bronson. "I'm sorry. It's just that sometimes . . ."

"I know." He reached for her hand and wrapped his around hers. "If it wasn't important, I wouldn't ask."

"I realize that." Dolly took a deep breath and began. "Casey was the sweetest, gentlest creature that ever walked on this earth. She had an innocence about her that would melt your heart." Dolly paused and her eyes glistened with tears. She half smiled, half cried. "When Casey graduated from high school, she . . . huh, insisted on going away to college. I told her it wasn't such a good idea, but she insisted. I suggested she move in with her cousin. I thought being family, they would watch out for one another." Carol lowered her head, but Bronson could still see the tears rolling down her cheeks.

He waited until she calmed down. "Go on," he urged.

Dolly shook herself. "Not much more to say. You know it all. She met that horrible boy and there was that party."

All of this, Bronson knew. He was hoping she'd remember some bit of information that would trigger his memory. He'd let her talk. Maybe if he got lucky . . . "What do you know about Harmon Moises?"

"Nothing you don't."

"Which is?"

Dolly shrugged. "I don't know. He supposedly gave Casey that date drug and she O.D'd."

"You said *supposedly*. Why the doubt?"

"Because you doubt it, and I trust your feelings."

Not much help there. Perhaps if they pursued another line of thinking. "Tell me about Eleanor Jorgeson."

"She's my niece and was thrilled when I suggested she and Casey room together. She's the one who introduced Casey to all of those fraternity boys. Afterwards, she felt so guilty. She blamed herself for Casey's death."

"Do you blame her?"

Dolly sighed and looked past Bronson as though she had caught a glimpse into the past. "It's irrational, I know. But yes, in a way, I do."

"And why's that?"

"She was so much in love with that fraternity boy—the president. She didn't pay any attention to my Casey. Now Casey is dead, but I guess my niece also got what she deserved. They got married shortly after Casey's death."

Bronson had known that Eleanor loved Sydney Stockwell, but he hadn't known they'd gotten married. He retrieved his notebook and jotted down the new information.

"Why would you say that Eleanor Stockwell got what she deserved?"

Dolly frowned. "Stockwell? Who's that?"

"The fraternity's president, Sydney Stockwell. Didn't you say Eleanor married him?"

Dolly's forehead furrowed. "Sydney Stockwell wasn't the president, was he? I always thought Ken Chalmers was. That's whom I'm talking about, Chalmers, the Texas senator."

Bronson flipped back the page and glanced at his notes. Trent had explained that Stockwell was the president in name but everyone followed Chalmers. When Bronson recorded that Eleanor was in love with the fraternity president, Bronson had made the mistake of assuming Eleanor was in love with Stockwell. "So Eleanor married Chalmers, but they obviously aren't still married. I've seen the current Mrs. Chalmers on TV and that certainly isn't Eleanor."

"No it isn't. The marriage—if you want to call it that— lasted less than a month. The pressure of Casey's death took a toll on them. And Sam always blamed you for that."

Bronson felt every muscle in his body stand at attention. "Who?"

Dolly looked surprised at Bronson's question. "Sam, Samantha. That's the new name Eleanor goes by. Shortly after her divorce, Sam went through a complete change. She cut and dyed her hair, changed her name to Samantha, and although I haven't seen her, I understand she gained a lot of weight. Didn't you know that?"

Bronson felt as if a bolt of lightning had hit him. A series of names flashed before him like a never-ending tape. *Sam = S. Eleanor = Ellie = L'ee. Eleanor Samantha Jorgeson became Eleanor Chalmers or L'ee Chalmers.* "You said she blames me for her failed marriage?"

"She more than blames you. She's down right bitter."

"Bitter enough to harm Carol?"

"What?" Dolly asked.

But Bronson was already running out the door.

Chapter 36

Bronson's heart drummed in his chest and his hands shook violently as he drove and whipped out his phone. He punched one and the number symbol, the shortcut to Carol's cell. "Come on. Pick up. Pick up." The machine connected him to her voice mail. "I love you," he said and flipped the phone shut.

He made it to Brick's in record time. He simultaneously turned off the engine and opened the door. He glanced at the parked cars and made a mental note as to their make and model.

Bronson stepped into the small entryway where a sign read Please Wait to be Seated. He ignored it and checked the dining area. No L'ee. No Carol.

He found the host. "Do you know L'ee Chalmers?"

The young woman frowned and shook her head. She seemed perturbed at the interruption to her schedule.

Before she could say anything else, Bronson added, "She's a rather, huh, large woman. Often needs help just gettin' along."

"No one like that has come in."

"Are you the only one who seats people?"

She nodded. "But the restaurant has another area. That's where the bar and smoking section are. We even have a dance floor."

Bronson couldn't imagine them being in that part of the

restaurant, but knew he should check anyway. "Where would that be?"

"Go as if you're going to the restrooms. You'll see a door to your left. That'll lead you into our smoking area."

Bronson thanked her and headed that way. Just as she had told him, as soon as he stepped into the small hallway, he saw a door to his left. He opened it.

The atmosphere in this part of the restaurant contrasted with the area he had just checked. Instantly, loud music bombarded him. A heavy smoker's cloud hovered over the area and Christmas lights lit the room. Bronson walked to the opposite end of the room. He didn't find them.

He ran back to the car. His fists pounded on the steering wheel. "Where are you? Where are you?" He had never felt so alone. So vulnerable.

He forced back the tears that threatened to erupt at any minute and was somewhat shocked that they were even there. He turned on the engine and headed toward the sheriff's office.

Through his office window, Quaid watched as Bronson pulled into the parking lot. Now what did he want? Filled with curiosity, Quaid headed for the reception area. The front door opened and Bronson rushed in. Quaid was taken by surprise. Somehow Bronson looked different. Defeated, maybe? He called him.

Bronson turned, saw Quaid, nodded, and headed in his direction.

Quaid didn't wait for Bronson. He knew the Dallas cop had something urgent to tell him and they would need some privacy. He led him to his office. As soon as he closed the door, Bronson blurted something out. Couldn't he wait at least until they had sat down? "What?"

"Carol, my wife—she's missin'."

"Missing?"

"Yeah, like gone. Disappeared."

He knew what missing meant, but decided not to point out the obvious. "How long has she been missing?"

"About an hour."

Quaid released the air he hadn't realized he'd been holding. "An hour? That's—"

"I know. Nothin'. She could be out shoppin'. Goin' out on a walk. Doin' the tourist bit, I know. I've heard it all. I've even said it a couple of times myself, but this time it's different. She's really missin'."

"How so?"

Bronson quickly but efficiently told Quaid about the events that had just transpired. Quaid reached for a pen and jotted down the main facts as Bronson stated them. When he finished speaking, Quaid put down his pen. He was silent for a moment, his thoughts still on the narrative. He knew Bronson was waiting for a solution, an answer, but he had none to give. "You're right. You've got reasons to worry and I'll help you any way I can, but don't you think it's a bit too soon to call in the state troopers?"

Bronson leaned forward, his eyes small pinpoints of anger. "What exactly does that mean?"

"It means that I'll do what I can. I'll put out a BOLO and contact the Safford police. This way they'll also be on the lookout. I'll need a description of the car they're driving."

"The hotel registration desk will have that information. I can ask a couple of the conference attendees to verify that information."

Always the detective. Didn't he remember he was supposed to be retired? "I appreciate the help, Bronson, but I'll put a couple of my deputies on that. You, better than anyone else, know the procedure. Go back home—in your case, the motel room—and wait for a call, in case L'ee Chalmers—or whomever—is trying to contact you."

"And that's it?" Bronson spoke between clenched teeth.

What did he expect? "No, that's not it." Quaid stood up. "I'm going to get you a recorder to attach to the motel phone." He walked out and returned a few minutes later. He handed Bronson the recorder. "Like I said, my hands are tied right now. You, yourself, said that she's been missing less than an hour and as it is, I'm sticking my neck way out for you."

"Right," Bronson said and walked out.

Chapter 37

On his way back to the motel, Bronson stopped by Brick's just in case L'ee had stopped somewhere else and had finally arrived. The host looked at Bronson and shook her head. He mouthed a *thank you* and checked anyway, knowing full well that they weren't there.

He returned to the car and thought about driving around, but until he knew the make and model of the car, there was no use.

Anxiety gnawed at him like a tiny insect nibbling on his insides. He had known sorrow and loneliness before. He had experienced fear and knew what it was like to be helpless. He had faced the darkness, the unknown, the enemy. It had all been a part of the job.

But this time, life had dealt him a blow he couldn't grasp. He bowed his head, closed his eyes, and for the first time in a long time, he whispered a prayer. He started the engine and headed toward the motel.

He approached the desk clerk on duty at the reception desk. "I need to see Wayne Weeks."

The youth nodded. "Yes, sir." He picked up the phone and informed Weeks someone wanted to see him. He hung up the phone and looked at Bronson. "He'll be right with you."

Less than a minute later Weeks approached. When he saw Bronson, his face broke out in a smile. "Good to see you,

Bron—" He stopped and stared at him. His eyebrows furrowed. "What's wrong?"

"I need to speak to you."

Weeks turned. "Let's go to my office."

As soon as Weeks closed the door, Bronson said, "My wife Carol has been kidnapped. I have reasons to believe that L'ee Chalmers is responsible. I need to know the make and model of her car."

Weeks leaned back in his seat and rubbed his chin. "Is this official police business?"

"You know better. You know I'm retired."

Weeks slowly nodded and looked away, as though deep in thought. He nodded once again, swung his chair toward the computer, and pressed some of its keys. "Problem is, it's against company rules to give out any information about our guests. You'd have to hand me a court order. Do you have one?"

Bronson looked down and shook his head.

"I see." Weeks tapped his computer. "Sometimes rules can be bent. Why don't I go talk to my supervisor, see if she'll give me permission to give you that information? I'll be gone three, four minutes." He tapped the computer and walked out.

Bronson waited for Weeks to close the door. He slowly counted to seven, stood up, and walked around Weeks' desk. He looked at the screen which showed L'ee Chalmer's registration information. Bronson retrieved his notebook, opened it to the proper page, and wrote down *Cadillac Deville, light platinum, Texas license plate CZM601.* He circled the word Texas and put a question mark next to it. Didn't L'ee say she was from Arizona? What was she doing with a Texas license plate?

He closed his notebook, put it in his shirt pocket, went back, and sat down. A moment later, the door opened and Weeks stepped in. "Couldn't find her," he said.

Bronson stood up and offered him his hand. "No problem. I'm sure I can get the information elsewhere."

"You do that." They shook hands and exchanged smiles. Bronson mouthed a *thank you* and as a response, Weeks nodded once. Bronson walked out.

Now that he had the information he needed, he itched to go out and cruise around. They could have changed their mind and gone to a different restaurant. It could be that simple.

But darn if that sheriff wasn't right. He needed to stay in his hotel room just in case L'ee—or anyone else for that matter—called. Of course he did have his cell and if L'ee had Carol, L'ee would demand Carol give her his cell number. In fact, chances are the call would come from the cell, making the call harder to trace.

Still, he should at least check his room for a note slipped under the door or a blinking light on the phone. Bronson bypassed the elevators—they took too long to arrive—and instead used the stairway.

By the time he reached the fourth floor, Bronson's air came in short gasps. Age had caught up with him. He and Carol had planned to spend their golden years together and now . . . now . . .

He quickly changed his line of thought. It wasn't age catching up with him. It was lack of exercise. He'd have to get himself on some type of daily exercise routine.

He reached the motel room and stared at the door. It didn't look like anyone had tampered with the lock. He looked down. He couldn't see any partial piece of paper sticking out. Maybe when he opened the door. He opened it, looked down, and saw nothing. No note shoved under the door. No blinking light on the phone.

No Carol.

He felt the empty, hollow stab of depression settle in.

A knock at the door sent a chill running down Bronson's spine. Automatically, he reached for his gun. It was still in the trunk of the car. Damn.

He peeked through the peephole. Lupe stood, wringing her hands, looking as scared as Bronson felt. He swung the door open.

"Mr. Policeman, I need to talk to you." Her lips trembled. Bronson let her in.

She started talking even before she entered the room. "I'm so sorry." Big tears ran down her cheeks. "She told me she was your wife. I let her in." A big sob shook her body.

"Who did you let in?"

"That woman. She said she was your wife. She said you needed towels. I'd forgotten to bring some. I was sure I had. But I brought some more anyway. She made me open the door. I really thought she was your wife. How was I supposed to know she wasn't? Please." She looked at Bronson with huge, brown, round eyes. "Please don't have me fired. My b-baby."

"I won't let anyone fire you. It's okay. You didn't know. Everyone makes mistakes."

Lupe's shoulders dropped with relief. She looked timidly at Bronson and attempted a smile.

"This lady who claimed to be my wife, what did she look like?"

"She was big. Huge."

L'ee! Bronson nodded. If only Lupe had told him this earlier, Carol would be safe now. Rage mixed with bitterness consumed Bronson. He opened his mouth, thought about it, and closed it. He bit his tongue to keep from screaming at the pregnant maid. He took a deep breath. When he felt he could trust himself, he said, "Thank you for comin'. I know exactly who you're talkin' about." He reached for his wallet and took out a twenty-dollar bill and handed it to Lupe. "For the baby. An early gift."

Lupe smiled in spite of the tears streaming down her face. "Thank you, Mr. Policeman. Thank you."

Bronson led her out. "If you see this woman who claimed to be my wife, please contact me immediately. Do you still have my cell number?"

She nodded.

Bronson closed the door behind her. The resentment inside of him felt thick and heavy, like motor oil after ten thousand miles. He slammed his fist against the palm of his hand. Dammit. Dammit all to hell. Why hadn't he insisted on talking to Lupe earlier? Why had he waited? Now it may be too late.

Oh God, was it too late for Carol?

He stopped. Destructive thinking never helped anyone. Now, more than ever, he had to focus.

Keep busy. Get moving.

He retrieved the recorder from its box and attached it to the phone. It was ready to use, but doubtful it'd be useful. He picked up the phone and asked to be connected to Gerri Balter's room.

Gerri picked up the phone on the third ring. "Hello?" Her voice sounded slurred, as though she had been asleep.

"Gerri?"

"Yes."

"Bronson. Did I wake you?"

"Yes, but it's okay. I was just taking a little catnap. It was time for me to get up anyway. What's going on?"

"Would you by any chance know what kind of a car L'ee Chalmers drives?"

"Let me think . . . Oh yeah! How could I forget? It's one of those big, fancy cars. A Cadillac, I think, kind of a silver-white. Why do you ask?"

"Have you seen L'ee today?"

"Nope."

"You weren't going to meet her and Carol for lunch?"

"If I was, nobody told me about it."

"What can you tell me about L'ee?"

"Not much. She hosts this conference. Has been doing so for several years. She pretty much keeps to herself. I guess that's because each year she seems to gain more and more pounds. It's gotten so that she has to rely on Balthasar for just about everything. Why, Bronson? Why all the questions? What's going on?"

Bronson closed his eyes and pictured Balthasar. Big, powerful, towered over him. He could easily overpower Carol. Bronson felt panic grab at his chest. He forced himself to take deep breaths.

"Bronson? You still there?"

"Yes, I'm still here. Sorry. Any idea where I can find L'ee?" and Balthasar?

"None, why? What happened?"

"If you see L'ee, please notify me immediately. I can't find Carol. She and L'ee went out somewhere for lunch."

"What do you mean, you can't find Carol?"

"She's not where she's supposed to be."

"Have you tried her cell?"

"Yes, I called Carol, but the message just went to her voice mail."

"No, not Carol. Have you called L'ee at her cell?"

Bronson grabbed the notepad and pen by the phone. "You've got her number?"

"Sure do. She gave it out to everyone attending the conference. Didn't you get it?"

"Apparently not."

"Hold on. I'll get it."

Bronson heard her put the phone down. Seconds later, he heard her pick up the receiver.

"Here it is." She gave him the number. Bronson jotted it down, repeated it, thanked her, and hung up.

Just as he reached for his cell, it began to ring. The caller I.D. told him the number matched L'ee's number.

Chapter 38

They were definitely heading the wrong way. Carol sat up straighter and concentrated on her surroundings. "Where are we going?"

L'ee, who occupied the front passenger seat lowered the visor and looked at Carol through the mirror. "Friend of mine lives up here somewhere. Her daughter gave me a package to give to her. You don't mind if we stop and see her? It won't take more than a few minutes."

Carol relaxed. "No, of course not, but won't Gerri and Gay wonder where we are?"

"They called just before you arrived. They told me they'll be at least half an hour late, but now it looks like we're the ones who are going to be late. I better call them. Do you have your cell with you? I'm afraid I left mine back at the motel."

Carol opened her purse, retrieved her phone, checked to make sure it was on, and handed it to L'ee who made no effort to contact their friends. Carol frowned.

"No service," L'ee said as she watched Carol through the mirror. "Maybe when we reach the top of the cliff, I'll try then."

Carol nodded. She had looked at her phone and could have sworn that she had three or four service bars. That meant she had a strong signal. Strange that L'ee would say she had no service. Maybe up here in the mountains, service drifted in and out. She leaned back and looked out the window. Instinct told her to pay close attention to the road and its landmarks, but the shadowy stretch of the woods prevented her from making any headway. One tree looked like the other. One road similar to the next.

Carol spotted a cabin and she breathed easier. That must be L'ee's friend's cabin. The car stopped in front of the cabin and Balthasar opened Carol's door.

Carol smiled. "I'll wait here."

"Get out."

The look in Balthasar's eyes filled Carol with apprehension. She looked at L'ee, seeking an explanation.

"You better do as he says," L'ee said.

As soon as Carol slid out of the car, Balthasar grabbed her and dragged her into the cabin.

"What the—"

"Shut up."

They entered the cabin and Carol's eyes focused on the chain strapped to the bed. She felt her heart jump to her throat.

Balthasar pulled her toward the bed and Carol let out an involuntary tremor.

Bronson forced himself to let the phone ring a couple of times before he answered it. "Bronson speaking." That was stupid. He should have just said hello.

"Hello, Detective Bronson, do you know who this is?"

The question threw Bronson for a loop. Kidnappers didn't normally want to be identified. "I may be wrong, but your voice sounds like L'ee's. How's lunch going? Do you need me to pick Carol up?"

The laughter at the other end of the line was laced with sarcasm. "Hardly."

A pause followed. Bronson waited.

L'ee continued, "You haven't figured it out yet, have you?"

"I've figured out a lot of things. It all depends on what you're talking about." It took a lot of self-control to keep from yelling at her and demanding to know what she had done. He wanted to speak to Carol, to hold her, to know she was safe.

L'ee's stern voice rang out, "There's only one thing we need to talk about. I'm sure you have my cell number. Call me when—"

"Wait! I know you have Carol. Is she all right?" He shouldn't have asked, but he had to know.

"Is Carol all right?" L'ee's tone taunted him. "For the time being, yes, but what happens to her will depend on you."

"Can I speak to her?"

"In time, yes, but now is not the time."

"What do you want me to do?"

"Have you ever gone geocaching?"

"What?"

"Geocaching, the game. Ever done it?"

Bronson retrieved his notebook and scribbled down the highlights of the conversation. At least that much of his professional mind remained. "I'm not familiar with geocaching."

"Really? I'm surprised you haven't heard about it. It's taking the world by storm. The premise is simple. You go to the geocaching Web site. It lists thousands of geocaching locations all over the world. You copy down the coordinates and go look for the hidden treasures."

"The treasures?" Did she mean Carol?

"Yes, the treasures. They usually consist of items you can buy at any dollar store. The trinkets are placed in some kind of container that is hidden and can be found by following the coordinates the computer gives you. When you find the treasure, you can keep any items you want, but you'll need to add something else to replace them. There will be a log in the cache where the finder records whatever he wants, normally things like whether this was an easy or hard cache to find, comments about the terrain or the geocache itself. You then put everything back the same way you found it. It's now ready for the next person who goes looking for it."

"Interestin' game, but—"

"Oh yes, it's fascinating. It's a great way to get people outdoors, forces them to exercise, and have some fun."

"I'm sure you're not interested in me exercisin' or havin' fun. What is it that you really want?"

"What I want is for you to go buy a GPS unit. You will need it when you go geocaching."

"Where can I buy one?"

"That will be up to you. Use your resources. See what you can find."

"What do I do once I get the GPS?"

"Don't worry about that. I'll contact you. As of now, you have forty-three minutes to get one. That doesn't give you any time to go to Sheriff Quaid or anyone else along those lines. In fact, if you want to see Carol again, you'll play strictly by my rules. No police of any kind. Is that understood?"

"It's perfectly clear."

"Good, because so far, you've wasted ninety seconds. That means you're down to forty-one minutes. You have less than five hours to find Carol. If you don't find her in that time frame, well . . . I'm sure you know the end results. The clock is ticking and we're watching you."

Bronson looked at his watch, then at the cell. It read Call Ended.

Chapter 39

The policeman part of Bronson told him he had to notify the authorities. All kidnappers always had the same rule: no police. Of course, no police. It was the police who rescued the victim and apprehended the criminal. But could Quaid? Bronson had his doubts. Still, the procedure was embedded in him. He shouldn't even consider not calling the police.

Yet, there existed another part of him—the part that was not a policeman, but a man, a husband, a lover, a father. That part ordered him to play it by L'ee's rules. Carol's life depended on it. He couldn't—wouldn't—risk it.

Maybe later, he'd call Quaid, but not now. The policeman part urged him to reconsider. Doing this alone was stupid and reckless. He reached for the motel's notepad and wrote down:

Carol, my wife, has been kidnapped. All evidence points to L'ee Chalmers. She told me that she was watching me, so please no police, for now. She's got—needs—an accomplice. Balthasar, perhaps? Wants me to buy a GPS unit. Plans to send me geocaching. Don't know the purpose of that. She drives a light platinum Cadillac Deville, TX plate CZM601. Please look for the car and be on standby.

He read the note, added his cell number and name, folded

the paper and wrote down Tom and Marie O'Day. He re-folded it until it was small enough to fit in the palm of his hand.

He rushed out. Downstairs, he approached the desk clerk, the same young man who had been on duty when he talked to Weeks. As Bronson worked his way to the desk, his gaze searched the motel lobby. It looked deserted. Not many places to hide.

"Do you know what a GPS unit is?" Bronson asked the clerk.

"Yes, sir. Me and my friends do some geocaching on my spare time. Joey—that's one of the guys in the group—has a GPS unit."

"Where can I buy one?" He couldn't help but look at his watch. He had wasted five minutes already.

"One of the pawn shops around town might have one. That'll probably be the cheapest place."

"Money is no object. Time is. Where's the fastest place?" What if he didn't make the deadline? He placed both hands on the countertop and opened his hands.

"That would be Wal-Mart."

"Where's the Wal-Mart?"

"As you leave the parking lot, turn right. Stay on that road—that'll be Highway 70. Toward the edge of town, you'll see it to your left. Can't miss it."

"Thank you." Without moving his head, Bronson surveyed the area as well as he could. They seemed to be alone. Still, Bronson lowered his voice. "Under my left hand, there's a note for Tom and Marie O'Day. Under my right hand, there's a five-dollar bill. It's very important that the O'Days get this note. Somebody may be watching us, so wait a few minutes after I leave to retrieve the note. Thanks for helping out." He turned and walked out, wishing the clerk hadn't acted so surprised. Hopefully, whoever was watching him hadn't noticed the youth's reaction.

Bronson walked out of Wal-Mart, bag in hand. He opened the trunk, supposedly to put the bag there. Instead, as unobtrusively as possible, he retrieved the five-shot, snub-nosed revolver and the box of ammo. He slipped them inside the Wal-Mart bag and slammed the trunk shut.

He looked at his watch. He had accomplished the task and had three minutes to spare. He folded his arms in front of him and leaned against the car. He watched the people coming in and out of Wal-Mart. None seemed to pay attention to him.

His phone rang. He flipped it open. L'ee calling. "Yes?"

"Good job, Detective Bronson. I assume you've got the GPS unit. That's what's in that Wal-Mart bag, isn't it?"

Bronson's gaze scoped the parking lot. No one stood out. Everyone seemed to be minding their own business. "Now that I have it, what do I do?"

"Now you'll go geocaching. Since this is your first geocache, I'm breaking you in nice and easy. Unfortunately, I can't send you to a computer to look up the information on this particular cache. After all, this cache was created just for you."

"I feel very special."

L'ee laughed. "I'm glad to see you're able to maintain your good sense of humor. I wonder how long that will last. I'm going to give you all of the information you'll need to find your first geocache. Do you have a piece of paper handy?"

Bronson retrieved his notebook and pen from his shirt pocket. "I'm ready."

"The Safford City Park hosts your first geocache. The coordinates are N32° 50.067 and W109° 43.207. This is an easy find, so you only have forty-five minutes. The clock is ticking. All the information you need is in the geocache. Good luck. I'd hate to have something happen to Carol before the four hours she has left are up."

The call ended and Bronson opened the trunk and retrieved the Wal-Mart bag. Once inside the car, he took the gun out, loaded it, and placed it in his waistband under his pullover Polo shirt. He started to drive out of the parking lot and realized he didn't know where he was going. He saw a woman with two small children. He rolled down the window and said, "Excuse me."

A worry frown creased her forehead. She reached for her children's hands. "Yes?" She took a step backward.

"Do you know where the Safford City Park is?"

She relaxed and gave him instructions. He thanked her, drove off, and glanced at his watch.

He had thirty-seven minutes to accomplish this first task.

In its prime, the cabin must have been luxurious, but neglect had taken its toll. The upholstery on the chairs and sofa had faded to a dull brown and had worn away in several spots. A thin layer of dust coated the furniture and impregnated the heavy, satin drapes. The place now stood dingy and poorly lit which, in a way, provided Carol with a bit of comfort. At least her captors couldn't see the fear in her eyes.

They also wouldn't spot the bit of hope she clung onto. She had memorized every bit of the cabin's layout and maybe that knowledge would help her escape.

That thought brought a new sense of fear. If by some chance such opportunity arose, would she ever be able to find her way back to safety? She doubted it. It seemed they drove forever to reach this isolated place.

More out of desperation and wanting to keep her mind

busy, she began to listen to the creature sounds outside the cabin. Somehow they sounded guttural. Unreal. Menacing. A shiver ran down Carol's back.

Chapter 40

Either the instructions the lady gave Bronson were extremely good or the park was easy to access. Either way, Bronson felt thankful when he saw the park. He drove past the rodeo barns and pulled into the parking lot.

As he parked the car, he scanned the area. For a Tuesday afternoon, the park bristled with activity. A group of elderly people packed the benches and jabbered nonstop to each other. Or maybe to themselves, Bronson couldn't tell. Two couples sprawled on the grass while their children darted between the trees. A teen, wearing a skimpy top and tight shorts that didn't quite cover all of her, moved to a rhythm only she could hear on her stereo headset. Bronson wondered why she wasn't in school, but then, with an outfit like that, it was a good thing she wasn't.

Bronson retrieved the GPS and took a reading. He was off by several degrees. If he headed west, he would find the correct longitude. He walked until the GPS told him he had reached W109 degrees.

He headed north, looking for the right latitude. That led him up toward a creek and a footbridge. Halfway across the bridge, he stopped. According to the GPS, he was standing right on top of the treasure. How could that be? He looked around and spotted nothing unusual.

The rail—maybe there was something attached to the rail. He checked. Nothing. The opposite side, then. Again, the search proved fruitless.

That meant that the only other place the treasure could be hidden was on the bridge itself, or more likely, under the bridge. He had two choices. Get in the water and look under the bridge or lie down on the bridge and try to see under it. The dry approach appealed to him more.

He lay on his stomach and looked under the bridge. He saw an envelope. Four thumbtacks, one in each corner of the envelope, held it under the bridge. Bronson reached for the envelope.

He sat up and ripped the envelope open. He noticed his hand shaking as he unfolded the note. It read:

Congratulations, genius.

You've actually mastered the skill of geocaching. Then again, this was such an easy find. Let's see how you do on a real geocache.

Your next set of coordinates are N37° 50.261 and W109° 54.311. The location, you ask? Well, first tell me whom the eighteenth president of the United States was and what fort he was assigned to. There are somewhere between 191 to 266 reasons why you need to know that. Try listing 157 of these reasons. You do that and it might just lead you down the right f_ _ _ _ road to Carol's cabin.

By the way, the game began at 1:06. Carol's time runs out at 6:06. Do you think you'll be able to find her before then? Tell me, Detective Bronson, are you worried about time? If you find the next geocache within an hour's time, you're still on schedule.

Good luck—or should I say—good luck to Carol? Hmm . . .

Bronson couldn't help but look at his watch. It read 2:22.

He looked around. Damn. No public restroom. Of course not, dummy. This is a city park and few come equipped with any kind of facilities.

He drove to the first gasoline station, parked in front of the men's room and went inside. He locked the door and flipped open his phone. He punched in the numbers to the hotel and asked to be connected to the O'Days.

Marie picked up the phone in the second ring. "Hello?"

"Marie? Bronson."

"Bronson, thank God you called. Are you okay? We got your message. Is there anything you want us to do?"

"I'm worried to death, and yes, there's something you can do. Do you have access to the Internet?"

"We've got our laptop with us and it's got wireless connection."

"Good. I need to know who the eighteenth president of the United States was and what fort he was assigned to."

"I'll get on it right away. Tom's out in the field, driving around, seeing if he can locate the car. He's also made a couple of calls. See what he can dig up. Ahh, here it is. The eighteenth president of the United States was Ulysses S. Grant. Damn!"

Bronson felt panic tightening in his chest. "What? What's wrong?"

"Grant, you know, Commanding General of all of the Union Forces. I'm sure we're going to find a lot of battlefields and forts mentioned."

"Damn. Maybe one will trigger something. Would you mind checking?"

"No, of course not. What's this about?"

Bronson briefly explained about geocaching and the hints L'ee had left. "That information should lead me to the location of the next geocache."

213

"I don't see how. Good luck deciphering the message. From my end, I'll try to get that information as soon as possible. When I find it, do you want me to call?" Marie asked.

"I'm not sure if I'm being watched, but just in case I am, I sneaked into the men's room and that's where I'm calling from. Just to be on the safe side, I'll leave my phone on vibrate and I'll call you back. Also, let me have yours and Tom's cell numbers, just in case I need to get in touch with either of you."

She gave them to him. He entered the numbers in his cell phone, thanked her, disconnected, placed the phone back in his pocket, and walked out. He approached the gasoline attendant. "I need to know where there's a Barnes & Noble."

Her hand froze halfway to the cash register. "This is Safford, not Phoenix or even Tucson."

Damn. He knew that. Of course there would be no big-name bookstore here. "How about a Big Five Sporting Goods?"

She glared at him.

Bronson bit his tongue. "Does this town have a sportin' goods store?"

"Yes."

Bronson waited. She didn't say anything else. So okay, he hadn't asked her where it was. "How do I get there?"

"You know where downtown is?"

"I reckon." He had driven past it on his way to Dolly's.

"Well, it's there."

"And the name?"

She folded her arms and frowned. "It's Gayle Connely. Why do you want to know that?"

Bronson closed his eyes and shook his head. "I meant the name of the sportin' goods store."

"Oh." She turned red.

She should have. Bronson waited.

"It's the Gila River Outfitters, or just the Gila Outfitters. One or the other, for sure."

Bronson thanked her and jumped back into his car. As he worked his way downtown, his mind focused on the note. The eighteenth president: Grant. What fort was he assigned to? And if more than one, which one served as the clue? What were the 191 through 266 reasons he needed to know that and why should he know 157 of them? And finally, what was that about the f_ _ _ _ road?

Bronson turned onto Main. Thank heaven for small towns. Downtown wasn't much bigger than two blocks long. He quickly located Gila Outdoors—*not the for sure, Gila Outfitters*—but finding a parking space proved to be a problem. He ended up having to park on one of the streets off Main and trotting to the store.

As he swung the door open, he immediately located the sales clerk. "I need a topographical map of the area. Do you have one?"

"Yes, sir. We have an Arizona atlas and gazetteer that carries the topography of all of Arizona."

"I'll take it."

The clerk's eyebrows arched. "Don't you want to see it first?"

"No." He thought about it. "Yes. Let's take a look at the map of this area."

"Yes, sir." He opened the atlas and gazetteer to the right page and showed it to Bronson. He scanned the area surrounding Safford. One word on the map shouted at him: Grant. Fort Grant. Located approximately forty miles from Safford. Can be reached by driving south on Highway 191, then west on Highway 266, and finally up Farm Road 157. Rather clever, he thought and wished L'ee's creativity hadn't included kidnapping Carol. Bronson's stomach did a flip-flop. "How much do I owe you?" Bronson asked, attempting to calm his edgy nerves.

"It's fourteen ninety-five plus tax."

Bronson retrieved a twenty-dollar bill from his wallet and shoved it toward the sales clerk. "Keep the change." Map in hand, he ran out the door.

The distance between Fort Grant and Safford jumped out at him. Forty miles away!

Even if he traveled at sixty miles an hour that would leave him less than twenty minutes to locate the next geocache.

He was running out of time.

Chapter 41

As Bronson drove through the mind-dulling expanse of rabbit brush, greasewood, saltbush, sagebush, and the occasional scattered cacti, his mind focused on Carol. Once again, the turmoil about not notifying Quaid ate at him. Getting the police involved was the right thing to do. Why hadn't he done that? This was Carol's life he was talking about. The thought froze his blood and a chill covered him.

He turned west to Highway 266 and soon the parched, barren earth gave way to scrub pine. Carol loved trees, the forest, the lakes. Her idea of heaven would be a cabin by a lake surrounded by trees.

A cabin!

L'ee's note had mentioned Carol's cabin. Was she indeed being held in such a place?

He whipped out his cell and punched in the appropriate numbers. When he heard Marie O'Day answer, he said, "Marie? Bronson here. I found a town close to Safford called Fort Grant. I'm headin' that way right now. I think that's what L'ee meant when she asked what fort Grant served under. But, if you don't mind, keep on searchin', just in case there's more to it than that. However, I'd like you to switch priorities."

"To what?" The static on the line made it sound like *to hat.*

"L'ee's note mentioned something about Carol's cabin. That's probably another hint. Mind doin' a search for cabins?

Are there any stores, restaurants—whatever—in the area that contain the word cabin? Also, see if you can find the locations of any cabins, especially in the Fort Grant area." He heard Marie sigh.

A brief silence followed, then, "That's a big job. I'll get on it right away."

"Thanks, I really appreciate it. Any word from Tom?"

"Soon as he has something, he'll call."

"Okay, thanks." He disconnected and looked at his cell. He only had two power lines. He had been able to make out every word she said, but at times the static on the line had made it difficult to understand. He hoped that didn't mean that he was about to lose service.

No sooner had he set the phone down, than it began to ring. Bronson picked it up. The caller I.D. read Tom O'Day. "Hey, Tom. Bronson here. What have you got?"

"I located the Cadillac. It's been parked all of this time at the Wal-Mart parking lot. I've checked and doubled checked. L'ee's not here, nor is Balthasar. But I'll continue to keep an eye out. Maybe—I hope—somebody will come get the car."

A feeling of cold helplessness washed over Bronson. He should have contacted Quaid. Under any other circumstances, Bronson would have spotted the car in the parking lot. Instead, he'd been watching people. He hadn't been thinking like he should have. "Have you checked the car out?"

"I called the motel and verified that it's the one registered under L'ee's name. License numbers are the same. Is that what you mean?"

"Are there any cameras attached to the car? Maybe that's how they were watchin' me."

"I'll check, but I can't do a thorough search without blowing my cover."

"I understand."

"Bronson, there's something else."

Bronson braced himself. "Go on."

"I have a police contact back in California. I asked him to run a license check. It turns out that the Cadillac registered under L'ee's name back at the motel actually belongs to a Joe Simes, better known as Balthasar. L'ee drives a green Jeep Liberty which I remember seeing parked in the motel's parking lot. I've always wanted to buy one so naturally I noticed it, but I couldn't tell you if it's the same vehicle. At the time I spotted it, I didn't have the license number or a reason to check it out. One thing I can tell you, the car is not in the motel's parking lot. I don't know how long it's been gone."

A Jeep Liberty, an all-terrain vehicle. Just the kind that would be needed for this case. L'ee sure had thought of all the details. "Thanks, you've done well. I'll keep my eyes peeled for that car."

"Bronson, don't you think I should tell Quaid what's going on?"

"He's aware that Carol is missin'. He just doesn't know about the latest developments." The conflict Bronson felt formed a tight knot in the pit of his stomach. "Let me find this second geocache, then I'll be able to tell better what kind of game L'ee is playin'. As soon as I know, I'll call you. At that time, we can discuss whether we should turn to Quaid."

"I'll wait for your call."

Bronson disconnected and stepped on the gas pedal. He had the road much to himself. For that, he felt thankful. Soon the trees of the Pinaleon National Mountains Forest thinned until Bronson found himself back in the parched waste of desert land. His uneasy feeling mixed with the heat and the quiet suffocated him.

Carol. Oh, Carol. Be safe, my love. Please be safe.

Bronson spotted the sign for Farm Road 157. He slowed

down and turned right. He drove past Angel Field. Who in their right mind would ever put a so-called airport out here in the middle of nowhere?

He checked the reading on the GPS. The longitude was almost right. Unless the road made a drastic turn, this road should lead him to the correct longitude, maybe a mile or two ahead.

Bronson stared at the dilapidated sign announcing Fort Grant's village limits—if you could call it that. There wasn't even a gas station in sight. Only the hot, dry heat greeted him. Bronson ignored the oppressive warmth and took another reading off the GPS. He was almost right on target. He pulled over, walked the few feet until he got the correct longitude.

He headed west, searching now for the designated latitude. He stopped. The treasure was here. Where? A lizard flickered between the cacti and desiccated bushes. He looked under each shrub, between the rocks, on the bushes themselves. Nothing.

The cactus didn't—couldn't—hide much. He walked around them, his heart thumping all the way in his throat. The GPS told him it was here, somewhere within a few feet from him. Why wasn't he seeing it?

He stopped.

Think.

He looked around, studying each object. Observing the earth. Would L'ee have buried the cache? He had been at a sporting goods store. Why hadn't he thought of buying a shovel? He would use a rock, if he had to.

He concentrated on the land. Dried. Undisturbed. No one had been digging around here in a heck of a long time.

The bushes, then. He had checked them before. Should he spend the time double-checking? Maybe, but not now. He folded his arms and forced himself not to waste any valuable time looking at his watch.

Concentrate on the terrain. What unusual items can I see? A pile of rocks. More than likely, man made. Not nature made. His stomach twisted and turned as he moved the rocks.

Nothing.

Damn!

Don't give up. What else? What is it that I'm overlooking? It's here. It's got to be here someplace.

His gaze went from item to item, his thoughts turning and twisting like a never-ending river. A cactus. A bush. The rocks. A cactus. A—he stopped. His gaze went back to the cactus. Why did it look different?

He headed toward it, his pace increasing with each step he took. *My God! That's a plastic cactus. Darn good imitation.* He lifted it. In the spot that the cactus had occupied, he found a small box marked Geocache Number Two. He reached for it.

Chapter 42

Carol lost all track of time. She couldn't tell if she'd been here for hours or days. No, it had to be hours. Three, four hours? It didn't matter. Her husband would find her. Just give him time. He'll come.

She pulled at the chain—again—attached to her ankle. It was no use, no use, no use. She had pulled, she had wiggled, she had hit, jerked, done everything imaginable but the chain would not yield.

At least it was long enough for her to stare out the window. If she somehow managed to get away, she'd follow the tire tracks down the hill. As far as she could tell, there was no road leading to the cabin. How would Harry ever find her?

Loneliness and bitterness engulfed her until it became a physical pain. No! She wouldn't allow herself to dwell in self-pity. Think. What would Harry do under these circumstances?

She sat at the edge of the bed and memorized every item in the room. Its shape. Its size. Its location. Its usefulness as a defense weapon or a tool to escape.

Her hearing picked up a familiar sound. She focused. She concentrated. A motor. Someone was heading toward the cabin.

She felt as if she had just swallowed broken glass.

The first thing Bronson saw when he opened the box was Carol's wedding ring. Then the note. He read it.

Congratulations, Bronson,

 I knew you could do it. How long did it take? Or more important, how much time do you have left—or should I say, how much time does Carol have left?

Bronson glanced at his watch: 3:34. He had less than two and a half hours. He continued to read.

 Read any Patterson novels lately? I bought his latest in Mesa, AZ. I recommend you read all of his books. You'll need that information for your next geocache. The coordinates this time are N32° 49.321 and W110° 00.935.
 I won't waste my time wishing you luck on your search. After all, I want time to creep away from you. But before I go, there's one more thing. This time you found Carol's wedding ring. Will you find her finger in the next geocache?
 Fascinating concept, don't you think?

Bronson let out a sound that was half moan and half animal sound. His tongue jammed back into his throat as he looked at Carol's wedding band.

 Small droplets of blood spotted the ring.

Chapter 43

Deadly fear gripped Bronson as he bolted back to the car. He opened the atlas and gazetteer he had purchased and forced his mind to focus on the task at hand. His hand shook as he glanced at the note.

The words *Patterson* and *Mesa* jumped out at him but no numbers that indicated possible roads. He searched the area close to Fort Grant. A couple of miles further up, he located some nameless fishing spots. Could they be Patterson and Mesa?

He looked at the coordinates. A wide gap existed between the current ones and the ones that had brought him to Fort Grant. He extended his search.

Then he saw it: Patterson Mesa Rd., running east to west on the other side of the mountain. He studied the map. Damn, no roads connected one place to the other. He'd have to go clear back to Safford.

He simultaneously started the engine and slammed the door shut. He stepped on the gas pedal and watched the speedometer climb. He stole a peek at the dashboard clock. It read 3:41.

He had a bit over two hours to find Carol and almost one hour of that would be spent on the road. Why hadn't he followed procedure and notified Quaid? Maybe he could have provided him with a helicopter. Now he only had two hours to find Carol.

What if he missed the deadline? Would L'ee really kill Carol? Was she that bitter?

A piercing pain as if thousands of needles had been inserted in him racked his body. He whipped out his cell. He should have called Quaid a long time ago. He was about to punch in the first number when he realized he had no service.

Damn. Double damn.

He thought of Carol and a feeling of apprehension engulfed him. He thought of God and felt a little better.

The scenery flew by and one cactus blended into another. He pushed down further on the gas pedal. He drove dangerously close to losing control of the car.

Once he no longer had the road to himself, he slowed down to somewhere between seventy-five and eighty. He pushed it back up to eighty-five, hoping the highway patrol would stop him. Then he'd be able to get word to Quaid, but as luck would have it, no one stopped him.

As he approached Safford, he checked service availability on his cell. As soon as he'd get some, he would call the sheriff's department and ask to speak to Quaid. Less than five minutes later, the phone displayed three service bars. He punched in Quaid's office number.

"He's not in right now, but I can connect you to his voice mail, or I can take a message," said the dispatcher.

Bronson chose the voice mail. "Quaid? Bronson. L'ee Chalmers is the kidnapper. I have evidence that proves it. I could use a helicopter. Contact Tom O'Day. He has all of the details." Bronson gave him the phone number and hung up.

Next he called Tom. He filled him in on all the latest geocache information.

"How many more geocaches will L'ee Chalmers have you find before she tells you where Carol is?" Tom asked.

Bronson had wondered the same thing. What if all he was

doing was playing this game and it would never lead to Carol? Yet, he had no choice. He had no other leads. "No idea. I'm hopin' this is it, but nothin' tells me this is so. All I know is that I'm runnin' out of time."

"What can I do to help?"

"Get hold of Quaid. I don't think I'm being watched but just in case I am, have him stay in the background. After I reach this third geocache, maybe I'll know a bit more. I'll need a helicopter in case there's another geocache at the opposite side of the mountain and a car—preferably a four-wheel-drive vehicle—to travel those roads. Don't know if I'll lose cell connection again, but a handheld radio that'll connect me to the sheriff would be nice."

"I'll go hunt Quaid down and get that done ASAP. Anything else?"

Bronson thought for a moment. Traffic had forced him to slow down to the mid-seventies. He couldn't afford to waste more time. "Yes. I need a police escort to open the roads."

"Where are you?"

"Approximately twenty miles away from Safford, comin' in on Highway 191."

"Hang on, I'll contact Quaid about getting you that escort."

They hung up and Bronson cursed the dash clock. It read 4:13. He had made good time so far, but he still had to drive through Safford and the other tri-cities. He forced himself to ease down to seventy-five. When had he pushed it back up to the eighties?

Seven minutes later he spotted a sheriff's car parked on the side of the road. As Bronson approached, he watched the vehicle with interest. The deputy turned on his lights and siren and pulled in front of Bronson.

His escort had arrived. Bronson breathed easier. For a

second, he had considered the possibility of Quaid arresting him for interfering with an ongoing investigation.

Halfway through town, Bronson's cell buzzed. A cold, clammy fear gripped him. Did L'ee know he'd contacted the police? "Bronson speakin'."

"Bronson, Quaid. Tom filled me in. This is what I have. The coordinates L'ee Chalmers gave you are on Patterson Mesa Road and Farm Road 156. We didn't turn down the farm road just in case the area was under surveillance. But at least you know how far to go. That should save you some time. As you get ready to turn off the main road and onto Farm Road 156, you'll see a boulder to your right. Beside it, on the side away from the road, you'll see a handheld radio. L'ee doesn't know about it, so you can contact me any time by pushing the talk button, channel one. I also got a helicopter in the area on standby should you need it. Anything else?"

"Not that I can think of. I just want you to know that I'm grateful to you."

"Don't mention it. I'm just an officer helping out another. I could get into trouble for letting you do this, so don't mess up. Be careful out there."

"I hear ya."

A bit past Safford, Thatcher, and Puma—what the locals called the tri-cities—Bronson's escort turned off his siren and lights. He pulled over and Bronson continued.

He was on his own.

Bronson looked at the clock. Even with all this help, time had slipped away. He only had one hour and fifteen minutes left, and the clock continued to tick.

Chapter 44

Bronson spotted the sign for Farm Road 156. He slowed down, came to a stop, and took out the GPS unit. The readings fell right on target, just as Quaid had promised. He stepped out of the car, headed toward the boulder, and pretending to search for the geocache, he picked up the handheld radio and slipped it in his pants pocket.

Following the GPS readings, he walked down the farm road, then turned left. The scrub brush cleared and Bronson saw a miniature replica of Stonehenge. He studied the eight-inch-tall circular wall. A pile of stones lay in its center. If his memory served him right, large rocks similar to benches compromised the center of Stonehenge. This replica contained a pile of stones.

He scattered them and found an Altoid Tin. *God, please don't let me find Carol's finger.* He took a deep breath and opened the tin. He saw a note and Carol's watch, no finger. He breathed easier. He pocketed the watch and read the note.

> *Hey,*
>
> *Since you're reading this, that means you've gotten good at the game.*
>
> *Congratulations, but have you looked at the time? I bet it has just slipped away.*
>
> *What a shame.*

Bronson didn't bother to waste precious seconds by looking at his watch. Every single nerve in his body tingled with the awareness of time. He continued to read:

> *By now of course you've found Carol's watch. I got to thinking. I can chop off her finger, or I can do her entire hand. The hand is definitely better, don't you agree?*
>
> *But, oh, don't worry. I'll hand you her hand. Wow! I really like that expression: hand you her hand. Cute, eh?*
>
> *Anyway, you will definitely find it in the next geocache. No maybes.*
>
> *About that, but if you hurry, perhaps she won't bleed to death.*

Bronson felt his legs sway. He steadied himself. *She's bluffing. She's got to be bluffing.* He forced his mind back to the note:

> *Which takes us back to the next geocache.*

Damn it. How many more geocaches will there be? Will he ever find Carol in time?

> *The coordinates are N38° 27.316 and W109° 49.391. If you don't find this last geocache, you'll be a real turkey and will fall flat on your face.*

The word *last* jumped out. *Last geocache.* Is this the one where he will find Carol? But L'ee hadn't mentioned finding Carol, only her hand. The thought filled him with fear.

He ran back to the car, took out the atlas and gazetteer, and looked at the coordinates: N38°. The coordinate by Fort Grant began with N37°. He began his search close to Fort

Grant. It didn't take him long to find it, Turkey Flat. As expected, no direct route existed. He would have to drive back to Safford then down Highway 191 to Road 366. According to the atlas, that road eventually deteriorated but it would take him to Turkey Flat. That meant at least another wasted hour on the road—or he could chance it and fly.

Bronson took out the handheld radio. "Bronson to Quaid."

"Quaid, go. What's going on?"

"There's one more geocache. Supposedly the last one. Coordinates are N38°27.316 and W109°49.391. That should put it on Turkey Flat."

"I'll have one of my men locate the general area like we did this last one. Anything else?"

"Yes, driving time is a little over an hour. That will put me there past the time I'm supposed to find Carol. I'll need to use a helicopter to get there."

"I'll have one pick you up in less than five minutes."

"Thank you. Over and out." Bronson stared at his watch: 5:03.

He had an hour and three minutes left.

He cursed time.

Chapter 45

Bronson and the pilot, an officer named Steve Paulson, had been in flight for a bit over fifteen minutes when Bronson heard Quaid's voice coming from the handheld radio. "Quaid to Bronson."

Bronson keyed the mike. "Bronson, go."

"You're right," came Quaid's voice over the radio. "The coordinates you gave me are indeed in Turkey Flat. I figure that if we drop you off on Trail 329, you'll have no more than a five-minute hike to the geocache's location." Quaid hesitated for a second, then added, "I hope you find your wife."

"Me, too."

Minutes later, the helicopter landed in its designated area. Bronson jumped out and ran down the road, closely following the GPS readings. He located the north coordinate and headed west. Several feet ahead, he came to the right readings and started his search.

No pile of rocks.

No Stonehenge. No plastic cactus or trees.

He walked around and searched the base of the trees.

Nothing.

Maybe he was looking in the wrong direction. L'ee could have put the geocache on top of the trees, in its branches. He walked around, looking up.

Still nothing.

With each passing second, Bronson's anxiety level grew.

Damn it! What was wrong with him? This was a simple game. Why couldn't he find the stupid geocache?

He stepped back, took a deep breath, closed his eyes, and forced his nerves to settle down. *Think logically. What do you see? What do you not see?* He opened his eyes and concentrated. He saw some ground plants, some oaks and pines. One mighty oak stood by itself. He'd begin with that one. He studied its base, then its trunk, and finally its branches. Nothing there.

He moved on to the next object.

A red squirrel, indigenous to only this part of the world, dashed from tree to tree. Bronson watched it and moved on to the next item. Three pines in a cluster. He compared their bases, their trunks, and their branches. Something caught his eye. The branches on the middle tree seemed unusual. Bronson hurried toward it.

As he approached it, he realized that those weren't pine needles. What was this branch doing sticking out of the middle of a pine tree? He pulled it out, revealing a hole in the almost-dead pine. He looked inside and saw a Tupperware container. He reached for it and pulled it out.

As he did, he realized the container was the right size to hold a hand. The plastic would, of course, prevent any blood from dripping out.

He reached for the lid.

And hesitated.

He couldn't open it.

He had to.

Oh, God. Help me.

Nervous fingers pried the lid open.

A see-through plastic bag revealed a hand.

Bronson dropped the geocache and let out a heart-wrenching moan that stemmed from deep within his gut.

Chapter 46

By now Carol had memorized every item in the tiny, one-room cabin. She had seen glasses and plates on top of the small kitchen counter. That probably meant that one of those cabinets contained a pot or a pan. They would make good weapons.

The problem that faced her centered on finding out which drawer contained what. "I'm getting hungry. Do you have anything to eat?"

L'ee turned away from her surveillance from the window. More than an hour ago, Balthasar had left and had not returned. L'ee looked worried. Her beady eyes flashed Carol a stern look. "What do you think this is? The Holiday Inn? I'm not about to prepare you a meal."

"No, but I could do it. I'm sure you're hungry, too."

"There's nothing to eat. Quit being a pest." She turned her attention back to the window.

So okay. She wouldn't find out which cabinet contained the pots and pans. At least not while L'ee was still here, and she didn't seem to have any plans of going away.

But Carol had found something else. Perhaps it wouldn't work as well as a pot or a pan, but at least it was something. An eighteen-inch-long branch rested against the fireplace. Its smaller branches had been cleared so that only stubs remained. This particular branch had obviously been used to stir the fire whenever the fireplace was used to warm the room.

The best thing about this branch was that it remained within reachable distance. At the first opportunity available, Carol planned to grab the branch and slip it under the bedspread of the metal bed she was chained to.

Maybe now would be a good time. L'ee seemed to be so preoccupied watching for Balthasar's arrival. Not that Carol didn't feel concern about that. As far as she knew, he had the only key to unlock her chain. She had watched him chain her ankle, then attach and lock the opposite end of the chain to the metal bed frame. He double-checked the locks to make sure they were secure, then slipped the key into his pants pocket.

Even if Carol managed to overpower L'ee, she still had to figure a way to unchain herself. Then, once outside, which way would she go? She assumed she'd be following the tire tracks, but what if Balthasar pursued her? She'd have to use the woods to hide. If so, she might get lost. She had never taken a survival course and she had no idea what to do. She felt the nerves in her stomach tighten into a knot.

Stop that! Harry would be so ashamed of me. He'd tell me to calm down and think logically. Carol drew in a long breath and slowly let it out. She silently counted to ten.

The anxiety attack vanished, or at least it went into hiding. *Get that branch.*

Carol began to pace, not toward the fireplace, but away from it.

L'ee turned around. "What are you doing?"

"I have a cramp in my leg. I'm just working it out." She continued to walk at a slow pace.

L'ee shrugged and turned her attention back to the window. "That's too bad," she said.

Carol increased her pacing area until it gradually included the fireplace. Without looking at the branch, she walked past the fireplace. As she did, she bent her knees, kept her back straight, and reached for it. Once she had it firmly in hand, she hid it between her arm and body and headed toward the bed.

She continuously watched L'ee who had her back turned and seemed not to pay any attention to her. Still, Carol chose to use caution.

Without changing the tempo of her pacing, she reached the bed. She sat down, quickly raised the bedspread, and placed the branch under it. She moved the pillow so that it concealed the bulge.

Her ears picked up the familiar sound of an approaching car. The last time she had heard the same noise, the sound level diminished instead of increasing. From that, Carol concluded that the vehicle traveled away from them. That gave Carol a bit of hope. Somewhere out there, nearby, a road existed and Carol promised herself to find it.

L'ee sat up straighter. "He's here."

Carol didn't know if the news brought her relief or tension. She sat at the edge of the bed, her attention focused on the doorway.

L'ee gasped.

As soon as Balthasar stepped in, Carol understood why L'ee had gasped. Balthasar stood in the doorframe, his right hand holding a gun.

Blind panic fueled Carol. She thought of the branch—what good would it do? Images flashed before her in fast succession. Harry's gentle face. The kids. The grandkids. Home. The camper. Would she ever see any of them again? She felt as if someone had reached into her insides and pulled them out. She closed her eyes and waited for the inevitable.

She barely heard L'ee give the command, "Balthasar, put that gun away. What do you think you're doing?"

Carol took in a deep breath. She wasn't going to die. She opened her eyes and saw Balthasar respond by raising the gun. A grin, filled with venom and defiance, covered his face.

He pulled the trigger.

Chapter 47

Bronson stood listening to his pulse beat loudly in his head. He stared at the hand enclosed in a plastic bag. He should have been more professional. He should never have dropped it—but this—this was Carol's hand. He blinked and stared some more. No, it wasn't. This wasn't Carol's hand—or anyone else's hand for that matter.

Bronson squatted and examined the item. The index finger rested on top of the middle finger, the universal symbol for hope. Was L'ee telling him there was hope for Carol? He examined the hand a bit closer. Its creator knew what he was doing. Very good wax imitation. *Dammit, L'ee, what game are you playing?*

Inside the bag, Bronson saw a note. He unfolded it and read it:

Congratulations.
You've found all four geocaches, but did you find Carol in time? I'm sure I don't need to remind you that time runs out at 6:06. I wonder what time it is now.

In spite of Bronson's strong will to ignore the time, his watch magnetized his eyes. He had less than thirty minutes. He felt the anxiety choke him. He continued to read:

Hope you kept all of the information from the other

geocaches. For there, you will find the answer that will lead you to your precious Carol—alive or dead, depending on what time you arrive.

Bronson frantically retrieved all four notes and re-read them. In his pocket notebook, he jotted down the names of the places where the geocaches had been hidden: Safford City Park, Fort Grant, Patterson Mesa Road, and Turkey Flat. He rearranged the words in different orders. He alphabetized them to see if the first letter of each word formed a new word. Nothing jumped out.

He checked his cell phone. No service.

He reached for the handheld radio. "Bronson to Quaid."

"Quaid, go."

"Marie O'Day is looking at cabin locations around this area. I need to know if she's found one that contains any of the following words: *Safford, city, park, fort, Grant, Patterson, Mesa, road, turkey,* and/or *flat.* Did you get all of that?"

"Got it. What's going on?"

"Found the fourth geocache. Note says I now have all of the information I need to find Carol."

"But?"

"I don't know what information that is."

"Hang on while I talk to my deputies." A slight pause followed. When he finished he once again spoke to Bronson. "Did you, huh, find . . . . L'ee said she'd, huh. . . ."

"I found a wax hand in the geocache. Scared the hell out of me when I first saw it."

"So she was bluffing."

"Yeah, I guess. All I know is that I have less than half an hour to find Carol alive—and I think L'ee isn't bluffing on this one."

"Then let's find her. I've got Marie O'Day on the line. I've already had one of my men explain to her what you need. I'll put her through."

No sooner had Quaid finished talking than Marie O'Day blurted out, "Sorry, Bronson, none of those words rings a bell. I looked at the street names, names of establishments, and even owners with that name or nickname. Can you think of anything I may be overlooking?"

He couldn't. He thanked her and she promised she'd continue looking. Quaid disconnected them.

"Now what?" Quaid asked.

"The answer is here, somewhere in front of my face. You've got the same information I do. Maybe one of us . . ."

"I'll do what I can over here. If I find something, I'll call. You do the same."

"Of course." Bronson moved his finger away from the mike and put the radio away. He opened his notebook to a clean page and drew four dots that represented the geocaches' approximate locations. If he connected the dots, they formed a trapezoid. He stepped back and looked at the figure. It didn't mean a thing to him.

What else? Think. Think. Time is runnin' out. If he connected dots one and two and dots three and four in the order of the geocaches, it formed a giant *X*.

He focused and images flashed in rapid succession before his eyes. He had found the first geocache in the middle of the bridge. A plastic cactus between two bushes held the second geocache. The third geocache consisted of a miniature Stonehenge. At its center, he had found the information. He had found the last geocache among a cluster of pines. The middle one had the fake limb.

All geocaches had been hidden in the middle—no, the center.

The fingers on the wax hand had been crossed, not telling

him there was hope as he had originally thought. The fingers formed an *X*.

X marks the spot.

At the center where the lines met—that revealed the cabin's location. He felt it. He knew it. He buzzed Quaid and explained his theory. Quaid put him on hold while he had his men do a quick calculation. A minute later, Quaid's voice came over the radio, "That places the cabin at the top of the mountain. The bad news is that area is heavily wooded and there's no place for a helicopter to land. This is strictly a car geocache. Good news is that the road leading to the top begins at Turkey Flat, and you're already there."

"How long of a drive before I get to the cabin?"

"Depending on the cabin's exact location, it's maybe a thirty- or forty-mile drive."

"Damn! Even if I do sixty. . . ."

"Don't count on it. It's a narrow, winding road."

All hope of finding Carol alive evaporated. The fear and anxiety that grabbed him choked him and left him feeling helpless. "We don't even know which cabin it is."

"I've got my men working with Marie. You'll soon have some coordinates."

"The car. Where's the car?"

"Should be there any second now. One of my men—"

"I see it." Bronson bolted toward it. He wanted to yank the driver out but instead waited until he brought the car to a stop. Bronson recognized him. He was the same deputy who had been assigned to make sure Bronson didn't leave Quaid's office. "You're familiar with these roads?"

"Yes, sir."

Bronson climbed into the passenger's side. "Good. Then drive like hell. I'll let you know when it's time to stop."

Bronson briefly looked around. Under normal circumstances, the beauty of the forest would have enthralled him. Instead, the deep shadows cast by the gigantic pines deepened his sense of dread.

"It's a real pleasure to meet you, sir. Your reputation follows you all the way to Safford. I know we sort of met before, but not officially. I'm Jonathan Welk."

"Nice to meet you, Welk, and nice of you to come."

"It's part of my job, sir. But even if it wasn't, I would have come anyway."

"I appreciate that." He keyed the mike. "Bronson to Quaid."

"Quaid, go."

"We're rollin'."

"I thought so. While I was waiting for you to check in, I got the coordinates. Do you have something to jot them down with or are you driving?"

"Welk's drivin'. Let me have 'em."

Quaid gave them to him and Bronson repeated them. "By the way," Quaid added, "I gave Marie the coordinates and she found a cabin located just on the spot. Belongs to an elderly local man. I've sent some deputies to go talk to him. Soon as I have anything, I'll call you. In the meantime, be careful out there. No need to kill yourself or my deputy. You probably noticed by now, the road is rather steep."

Bronson watched as Welk maneuvered another hairpin curve. "So I've noticed."

"Me and some deputies are heading your way. We're maybe fifteen, twenty minutes behind you."

"Fine."

"If nothing else, we can meet at the cabin."

If it is the right cabin. God, what if I'm wrong?

There were no guarantees—even one that said he'd find Carol alive.

The thought pulled at Bronson's heart.

Chapter 48

Apprehension gnawed at Bronson's nerves, eating slowly away at his resolution. They had been on the road now for fifteen minutes and they were nowhere near where the GPS told him he should be.

Time both froze and sped up. The dashboard clock told him he had nine minutes left. "Can't this car go any faster?"

Welk pressed down on the accelerator and Bronson prayed they wouldn't encounter another car on the next curve. Outside, the birds shrieked and the shadowy stretch of the woods cast eerie shapes.

Bronson shook himself. No more self-doubts. He'd never be able to help Carol under those circumstances. He would reach her in time. He had to.

He checked the GPS. He had reached the first coordinate. "We're here. Pull over."

Welk did and they got out. Bronson's gaze scoped the hill, but he couldn't see any cabins. Quaid and Marie had assured him one would be up there. He believed them. "I'll cover this side of the mountain." Bronson made a sweeping motion with his arm to the right side of the mountain. "You cover that side. One of us finds something, he'll call the other."

Welk nodded and began his ascent.

Keeping low and using the trees as cover, Bronson also began to climb the hill. As he headed upwards, he reached for his gun, reassuring himself that he had easy access to it. He pushed on. The deathly silence of the forest caused his heart to pound extra hard. He felt sure it would give him away.

Not wanting to but unable to stop himself, he stole a glance at his watch. Three minutes left. The anguish he felt pushed him harder up the hill. The cool shadows, mixed with his fear, caused him to shiver.

Between the trees the faint outline of a cabin took shape. Bronson paused long enough to assess the situation. It looked deserted. Still, he scoped the surrounding woods. He looked for the glint of a reflected light from a gun or a rifle. He observed the shapes, looking for a possible place for a sniper to hide.

Failing to see either, he crouched lower and radioed Welk the information.

"I'll be there as soon as possible," Welk said. "Over and out." Bronson imagined Welk moving toward the cabin even as he spoke.

Rationally, Bronson knew he should wait for Welk. Every policeman needed a backup, a partner. But that would require time, and time was not a luxury Bronson had. As he advanced, he looked at his watch. The time read 6:07.

Bronson's heart did a flip-flop. He had missed the deadline. His mouth felt as dry as if it had been stuffed with cotton. Carol would be all right. He had to believe that. He was going to reach her in time, but he wouldn't get there unless he was careful. He reconsidered his options.

Chances were that L'ee, Balthasar, and anybody L'ee might have hired would be expecting him to approach from the front of the cabin. Their guns, their focus would be directed toward that area. He needed the element of surprise. He changed direction and headed in an arc shape and approached the cabin from the side. He moved quickly and efficiently, like a lion on a hunt.

His mind, his soul, his every essence focused on the cabin and getting Carol out alive. He expected to find Balthasar and perhaps some others crouching behind the pine trees, rifles ready, waiting for Bronson to make his appearance.

Instead, he found no snipers. With cat-like movements and keeping as low as possible, he reached the edge of the cabin. Still, he saw no one. The hairs behind his neck stood up. *Behind me. They must be watchin' me creep along. Why haven't they shot me?* He executed a one-hundred-and-eighty-degree turn, whipped out his gun, raised it, and aimed it at . . . nothing.

The stillness of the forest filled him with dread. Where was Balthasar? What was he planning? Bronson plastered his body against the cabin wall and worked his way toward a window. As unobtrusively as possible, he peeked in. He saw a one-room cabin consisting of a kitchen area, a sleeping area, and a living area. The place looked deserted. Yet the GPS told him this was the correct location. Had he been wrong and misread the clues?

Bronson scooted under the window and worked his way toward the door. It stood open. Not a good sign, he thought. He braced himself, squatted, and stuck his head in just far enough to see.

He gasped.

Chapter 49

"Spread out. Spread out," Quaid ordered his men. They had reached Turkey Flat in what Quaid considered record time. "I want every inch of the mountain covered. Anybody going up or down won't be able to get past us. We'll make sure of that. Is that understood?"

Some men mumbled a *yes* while others nodded.

Quaid looked at the men. "Be careful out there and good luck. Do any of you have any questions?"

No one had any. "All right, then go, and don't forget to keep in constant touch. I don't want any surprises." Quaid watched the deputies ascend the hill. On his way to Turkey Flat, he had decided it would be best if he stayed at the bottom and coordinated the effort from there. As he watched the men disappear up the hill, his heart filled with doubts.

He could just as easily make decisions from the top as well as the bottom. Besides, if he started now, he'd be closer to the action.

Bronson entered the cabin, swinging his gun in a wide arc, while scanning the room for Balthasar or any other dangers.

"You look . . . ridiculous. . . . Put the gun . . . away. It's just you . . . and me," L'ee said. "No one else."

Bronson stood up and headed toward L'ee. She had been shot in the chest two times, and the wounds bled profusely.

L'ee had placed her hands over the primary wound in a futile effort to slow the bleeding.

Bronson bent down and examined the wounds. One was superficial and was close to the shoulder. The other one, a sucking chest wound. He retrieved the radio.

"Put that away," L'ee ordered.

"I'm going to call an ambulance for you."

"If you want to know . . . where Carol is . . . put that away."

Bronson returned the radio to his pocket. "Go on."

"Sit down. . . . It may take a while."

Just tell me where Carol is. He sat on the floor next to L'ee. "Is she all right?"

L'ee stared at him intently and remained quiet. "I'll begin at the beginning."

Just tell me where Carol is. From the corner of his eye, he saw someone approach. He put his index finger to his lip, telling L'ee to remain quiet. He lay flat on the floor, his gun pointed at the door.

Welk stepped in, half crouching, gun pointing.

Both Bronson and Welk simultaneously let out sighs of relief. Bronson turned to L'ee, "You were sayin'?"

"I'm dying of cancer."

Bronson knew he should say something, but nothing appropriate came to mind.

L'ee continued, "I know I look . . . healthy, but in a couple of months . . . I'll be . . . dead. So I chose this instead."

"But why Carol? What did she ever do to you?"

"Nothing. In fact, I like her."

Like—as in the present tense. A sense of relief flooded through Bronson's veins.

"It's you . . . I wanted to punish." L'ee's voice filled with venom. "You're . . . the one . . . who ruined . . . my marriage.

You're the one . . . who ruined my life. . . . Look at me now. . . . I'm grossly fat and . . . ugly. All because of you."

Bronson failed to see how he had ruined L'ee's life, but under the circumstances, he wasn't going to debate it. "I'm sorry you feel this way." He wanted to hear about Carol, but he knew that the more he asked, the less likely she'd be to mention her.

"My marriage—if you want to call it that—" L'ee paused and took in a deep breath. The pain registered in her eyes. "Ken and I were married . . . for less than . . . a month. Then he . . . filed for divorce. He thought . . . with Casey's murder . . . her being my roommate . . . it would bring him disgrace. Now look at him. . . . He's a senator . . . possibly the next President. I could have been a . . . first lady. Instead, I became this." She removed her hand from the wound long enough to make a sweeping motion of her body.

"Tell me about Balthasar."

"He betrayed me."

"How? Where is he now?" *Where's Carol? Is she all right?*

"You're getting . . . ahead of the story. It all . . . began a year ago . . ."

Chapter 50

One year ago:
Papers about the convention hotel, flight costs, food costs, estimated income from the number of people expected to register, a must-do list—all of these lay scattered on L'ee's desk. The Slayers Convention would soon be here and she still had a lot of loose ends to tie up.

This one would be by far the best convention. After all, this was the one she'd be inviting Bronson to attend. She hadn't quite yet figured out how she'd accomplish that. All she knew was that she'd make sure Bronson attended. Other than that, she'd taken care of all the Bronson-related details, including writing the script that the Slayers were supposed to solve.

Her doorbell rang and L'ee felt the stirrings of anger. How dare someone disrupt her privacy. She swung the door open, half expecting to see a salesman. Instead, the well-dressed man with piercing brown eyes studied her. "Are you Eleanor Chalmers?"

"It's L'ee now. Are you a reporter?"

He wet his lips. "No, but I really need to talk to you." He looked behind him as though searching to see if anyone had followed him. "Please."

"What is this about?"

"Not here. I need to come in." He ran his fingers around the collar of his shirt as though it were choking him. "Please, it's really important and very personal."

L'ee hesitated for a moment before letting him in. She opened the door and led him into the living room. "If you're selling something—"

"I'm not. I'm here to share some information with you."

"What kind of information?"

"I've developed a secret passion for writing and mysteries, and all because of your ex, Ken, and Casey."

His statement intrigued L'ee. She stared at him and realized he looked almost frightened. She studied him intently. Then it dawned on her. "I know you."

"Yes. I'm Trent Powers."

Of course. "From the fraternity."

"Yes."

"Please sit down." She pointed to the couch.

He sat on the edge of the seat and without looking up he began. "I don't know if I'll have the courage to go through with this, so just let me get it all out." He took a deep breath. "Three people were involved in Casey's death: Sydney Stockwell—you remember him? He was the fraternity president—and me. The two of us were involved because we have known all along who the murderer is, and we covered up for him. Him, being your ex."

L'ee felt as if a giant rock had landed on her chest. "Ken? Why would he want to kill Casey? He barely knew her. I can't believe he'd do something like that."

"Believe it. Mr. Squeaky Clean has a lot of dirt to hide. In college, we made money by selling drugs to a select number of sorority and fraternity members. Casey found out about it and threatened to go to the police. She also planned to warn you not to marry Ken. But Ken was a lady's man, and he wasn't worried. He figured he'd seduce Casey, like he did all the other ladies. What he wasn't counting on was Casey's not accepting his advances. He pursued her and it intrigued him when she wouldn't reciprocate. He found her fascinating and doubled his efforts until one night after a lot of heavy drinking, he succeeded in making love to her. The next morning she felt horrible. She had betrayed you. She told Ken that she wasn't going to wait anymore. She would head to the police and then she'd pay you a visit. Ken pretended to feel shame and said he wanted to be the one to tell you. He convinced her that he wouldn't sell any more drugs if she didn't go to the police. Casey agreed, but Ken always knew that it would only be a matter of time before she told. That's why Casey had to die. In the end, Ken got what he wanted. With his lies, he had bought some time. He used it to set up her murder."

Tears of bitterness stung L'ee's eyes. "I don't believe you."

Trent remained quiet.

"Why are you telling me this now?"

"Ken plans to announce his candidacy for President of the United States. Chances are he'll win. A person like him shouldn't be allowed to be President."

"Why are you telling me this? Why not go to the police?"

"Two reasons." He raised his index finger. "One, Ken has a lot of people on his payroll. I'm not sure whom I could trust. Besides that, going to the police would implicate me. I don't want to do any time for this." He raised the index and middle fingers. "And two, I figured you could still get hold of Bronson. Ken did you wrong and I thought you'd like to have the opportunity to get even. You see, one of the reasons he left you is because you reminded him too much of Casey, and he was halfway in love with her when he married you. Still, he did marry you and would have stayed married had it not been for Bronson. Ken liked the idea of using your parents' money to further his career. But when Bronson started checking you out as a possible suspect, he panicked. That was too close to home. So he dropped you."

L'ee shook her head and fought hard to control the burst of anger she felt ready to erupt. "I knew that if Bronson kept hounding me as if I were the murderer, Ken would leave me." The resentment that had been building over the years surfaced and fueled her need for revenge. She remained quiet while her mind conceived a plan. She smiled and looked up at Trent. "Let me see if I have this straight. You told me Ken killed Casey and you want me to get hold of Bronson—whom you know I hate—so that he can arrest Ken. Is that about right?"

Trent squirmed in his seat, looked at the ground, and nodded.

"So if Bronson takes up the case, he'll suspect that maybe I've withheld evidence all of these years. I will end up in jail, and you, on the other hand, will come out smelling like a rose."

Trent's eyes opened wide. "That's not . . . I didn't think . . . I . . . I . . ." He shrugged and sank deeper into the couch.

"I can easily implicate you. You know that, don't you?"

He nodded. "Please don't. I don't want to go to jail."

"In that case, you will do exactly as I say. Is that understood?"

A look of uncertainty crossed Trent's eyes. "What is it that you want me to do?"

"There's a man by the name of Max Iles. In order for me to get hold of Bronson, Max must be removed."

Trent's eyes narrowed. He wet his lips. "What do you mean? Removed?"

"I could see him having some kind of an accident that would prevent him from doing his job."

Trent paused as though considering L'ee's words. "I fail to see the connection between Max and Bronson."

"And you don't have to see the connection. The less you know, the better. All I will tell you is that the only way for me to get Bronson is for Max to momentarily disappear. Do you think you can arrange that?"

For a long time, Trent remained quiet. Slowly he nodded. "I know someone who can arrange an accident—nothing more."

"An accident is all I need."

Chapter 51

It had taken a lot of effort to tell the story, but now that she had, somehow L'ee felt better. She took in a deep breath. "The accident . . . as you know . . . went wrong . . . and Max died . . . We . . . never . . . ." A tear escaped her eye. "There's more. . . . There's the part . . . you really want to hear."

Welk eyed Bronson and barely nodded an encouragement.

Bronson ignored him. Instead, he sat patiently listening, hoping to get a clue as to Carol's whereabouts. "I'm listenin'."

"Balthasar came in and shot me . . ."

"If I wanted you dead," Balthasar had told L'ee, "you'd be dead by now, but my boss, that'll be Senator Ken Chalmers, wanted you to know what was going on before you died. You thought you hired me to be your chauffeur and general gofer. But Senator Chalmers is paying me twice what you pay. He's been suspicious of Trent for quite a while. He's seen him grow soft and weak like a woman. The Senator learned about the conference so he sent a man who sometimes goes by the name of Norman Childes to silence Trent forever. You know Norman as Sydney Stockwell. Even while he was the fraternity president, he hated Trent. Always thought he had no backbone." He paused so L'ee could digest all of the information. "So now you know. The frat president, Sydney Stockwell, attended the conference under the name of Norman Childes, and he was the one who killed Trent. That's all I have to say. Do you have any questions before I kill you?"

From behind him, Carol crept toward Balthasar, holding the limb like a baseball bat. L'ee saw her and vaguely wished Carol wouldn't reach him until after Balthasar had the chance to shoot her. Dying from a bullet wound would be much quicker and less painful than dying from cancer. L'ee closed her eyes, anticipating the next shot.

It came at the same time that Carol whacked Balthasar in the head. The bullet meant to kill L'ee only wounded her. As Balthasar fell forward, his gun went off a second time. The bullet found its target in L'ee's chest. He landed unconscious on the floor.

Carol stared at L'ee, not sure as to what to do. L'ee swept the air with her hand, telling Carol to go away. Carol lost no time in searching Balthasar's pockets for the key. She found it in his right front pocket. She grabbed the key and freed herself from the chain that had held her prisoner. She reached for the discarded gun and looked at L'ee. "If I make it safely down the hill, I'll get you help." She ran out the door.

By now, L'ee could barely talk above a whisper. Her weakness told her death hovered nearby. She embraced it. "I . . . must . . . have passed . . . out."

Bronson looked up at Welk to see if he had heard. He shook his head. Bronson leaned closer so he could hear her.

"When . . . I came to . . . he . . . was gone. He . . . must . . . have . . . gone . . . after . . . Carol."

Bronson bolted for the door and spoke to Welk as he rushed out. "You stay here with her. Call Quaid. He's headin' up this way. Fill him in." He ran out. Once outside, he hesitated. Which way would Carol go? How close was

Balthasar to her? He retrieved the handheld radio as he sur-veyed the ground outside the cabin. He looked for broken twigs or any sign that would tell him which direction to go.

He raised the radio to his mouth. "Bronson to Quaid."

"Quaid, go."

"Where are you?"

"Not far from the cabin, I've got my men advancing up the hill. We're covering a wide perimeter of the mountain. How are things at your end?"

"You know about L'ee?"

"Welk reported in. Any word on Carol?"

"All I know is she's somewhere out here in the woods. Balthasar may be after her." Bronson stopped and bent down. He could barely make out a man's footprint. But it was there, nonetheless. The prints led up the hill, away from Quaid and his men.

Chapter 52

Sixteen Minutes Ago:
At first, Carol had hesitated as to which direction to head. She had escaped, but she wasn't yet safe. What would Harry tell her? *Do the unexpected.* If she headed down the hill that would be the way Balthasar would expect her to go.

She'd head up the hill, and then turn left and come back down. With luck, she'd encounter the road. Without further thought, she ascended the hill.

Bitch!
That little bitch had knocked him out and escaped. Balthasar rubbed his head. It hurt like hell, but at least she hadn't drawn any blood.

She'd be sorry for what she had done. He had planned to kill her quickly, using a single, carefully aimed shot. Now he'd let the bitch suffer.

Balthasar slowly sat up and the world spun. He closed his eyes while the pain subsided. He didn't know how long he'd been unconscious. Couldn't have been that long. He stood up and waited for his eyes to focus.

He saw L'ee's inert body. At least that had gone right. Every time she gave him an order, he cringed and counted the days until he'd be able to kill her.

He looked around for his gun. Gone. That bitch had probably taken it. He reached for his ankle and produced the handgun he had strapped to his leg. That stupid bitch hadn't even bothered to search him. Shows how stupid she is.

He stepped out. She'd probably follow the trail that would eventually lead to the road. He wouldn't allow that to happen. She may have had a head start, but he was agile. She was old and certainly out of shape. "I'm coming, bitch," he said and headed down the hill.

Carol ignored the stitch in her side and instead once again broke into a run. Her muscles protested, but she moved unthinkingly. She ran clumsily, dodging the fallen timber where she could and climbing over rotting trunks she could not avoid.

All she wanted was a place to rest, but where? Had she gone far enough? Her burning muscles begged her to stop, but if she did, would Balthasar find her? She knew she had to keep moving. Cold fingers of panic clutched her heart.

No, no. I mustn't panic. Just keep moving.

Just keep moving.

Balthasar didn't quite know when or where the thought hit him, but it made perfect sense. The bitch wouldn't head down the mountain. That's what she'd expect him to think. She'd do the opposite. She'd go up the cliff, away from danger. She'd travel in that direction for ten, fifteen minutes, then she'd make a sharp left. That should put her traveling parallel to the road. Once she had traveled in that direction for another ten minutes or so, she'd start downhill.

He bolted back up the cliff.

What the bitch didn't know was that he was an expert tracksman. He would use that skill to hunt her down. He returned to the cabin's front door and studied the ground. It didn't take him long to pick up her trail. Just as expected, she was moving up.

It wouldn't take him long to catch up with her. Then she'd pay. Oh, how she would pay.

Carol figured she had climbed high enough. She could now make a ninety-degree turn and travel west before working her way down. Maybe now she could slow down. Her heart felt like a pumped balloon on the brink of rupture. She needed to rest, but should she allow herself that luxury? Surely, she had outrun Balthasar by now.

If she closed her eyes, she could hear Harry's voice, "Don't ever assume anything." She hoped Balthasar hadn't regained consciousness. She hoped she had traveled far enough away from danger. She hoped . . . But she had no way of knowing.

Never assume anything.

Her bruised and tender heels became constant reminders of her predicament. She pushed on harder, faster.

Something changed and an involuntary tremor ignited deep within her. The tunnel of noise that had surrounded her came to an abrupt stop as though seeking refuge from a deadly predator. She paused, her head slightly tilted, her ears straining to listen.

The silence, like smoke, whirled and grasped at her raw nerves, causing her flesh to crawl. Her eyes darted from side to side. In a blaze of growing terror, Carol broke into a run. She breathed hard through her mouth. Her screaming lungs begged her to slow down, but she ignored them and forced herself to continue her flight.

She ran blindly through the woods, ignoring the fallen timbers, the rotting trunks, and the protruding boulders. She ran as if in a nightmare, her muscles on fire. She stumbled and a sob caught in her throat as she gasped for breath.

Luckily, she regained her balance and used that moment to steal a second to glance behind her. The woods stood as before, silent and threatening. She turned to continue her flight and froze.

Balthasar stood five feet away from her, evil emanating from his dark, brooding eyes. He held a gun and all Carol could see was the barrel pointing at her.

Chapter 53

"Hello, bitch," Balthasar's voice came like a whisper of graveyard breeze.

Carol felt panic tightening in her chest. She had to do something. She remembered the gun. She had put it in her belt like she had seen Harry do many times. She felt the belt with her arm. The gun was gone. It had probably fallen when she stumbled or when she ran in blind panic. She felt her body sag with bitter disappointment mixed with fear. Oh, Harry, where are you? She raised her head and stuck out her chin. "Hello, Balthasar."

"The name is Joe Simes. I hated L'ee for calling me Balthasar."

"I imagine she'll never call you that again."

"No, she won't and neither will you. Your life is over."

Carol screamed, a loud ear-piercing wail that stemmed from the pit of her stomach. "I always wanted to do that. Did it hurt your ears?" Her raw throat ached.

Balthasar's eyes pierced hers. "What were you hoping to accomplish with that scream? No one could possibly have heard you. We're here alone. Just you and me and this gun." He smiled, a cruel curvature of the lips that spoke of triumph.

Carol felt bitter with the knowledge that she had failed. She didn't want to die. Not today. Not like this. "I don't suppose you'd grant a dying woman a last wish."

"This isn't Candlelighters, but I want you to know I have nothing against you. I'm just doing my job."

Carol's breathing rate accelerated rapidly, as if she were hyperventilating. She saw him raise the gun. She closed her eyes. The explosion of the bullet deafened her. She started shaking, uncontrollably.

Someone held her. Called her name.

She tried to push away from the tight embrace. She had to get away. The grasp was tighter. The suffocation she felt caused her to gag.

"Carol!"

That voice!

"Carol, you're okay."

She tried to regain her breathing, tried to ignore the prickle of fear that drenched her body. She stared at the man holding her. Tears beamed in his eyes. Why was he crying? Who was he?

"Carol?"

She gasped. "Harry!"

He nodded as though she had asked a question.

"Oh, Harry." She gave in to the comfort of his arms.

"You're safe," he said as he stroked her hair and kissed her. He wouldn't stop kissing her, holding her.

Yes, she felt safe now. But Balthasar was going to kill her. "What happened?"

"You screamed and I heard you. I got here just in time to see Balthasar raise the gun. I shot him."

She looked toward the cluster of trees where Balthasar once stood. "Did you kill him?" She didn't want to know. She didn't want to see his fallen body. She purposely stared at her husband.

Bronson shook his head. "I know I wounded him, but he got away."

"Shouldn't you go after him?"

Bronson held her tighter. "No. I want to be with you. I want to hold you, make sure you're okay."

"I'm fine. If you need to go, go." She tried to straighten herself, attempting to look taller and stronger.

Again, Bronson shook his head. "Quaid's got men all over this mountain. They'll find Balthasar." Bronson looked at his wife's face and wiped her tears away. "Thank you, God, for giving me my Carol back."

She smiled and they kissed.

Chapter 54

"Amazing. You in church. Never thought I'd see the day," Carol said as Bronson opened the car door for her. The eleven o'clock service had just ended and Carol hoped her husband would take her out to eat.

After Carol settled in, Bronson closed the door and went to the driver's side. "When I realized you'd been kidnapped, my whole world seemed to end. I felt so lost, so empty. Don't ask me why I did it, but I asked God to keep you safe. By going to church, I'm officially thankin' Him."

Carol placed her palms on his cheeks and kissed his lips. "That's the sweetest thing you've said."

Bronson smiled and looked out the car window. The day promised to be another warm one. Already the heat waves rose from the bare earth. Bronson turned on the engine and the air conditioner. "Glad you feel that way because you probably won't like the next thing I have to say."

Carol rolled her eyes. "Here we go again. What is it this time?"

"I'm goin' to go see Quaid." Bronson pulled out of the parking lot.

"Now? On a Sunday?"

"He's on duty. You ought to know that."

Yes, of course she knew that. Policemen—even retired ones—are always on duty, but couldn't he wait at least until after lunch? "This is our first day after that horrible event."

Bronson frowned and looked apologetic. For a minute, Carol thought Harry would actually give in. Then he took a deep breath and Carol knew it was over. "I know, sweetheart, but I need to get this wrapped up. I really should have gone yesterday, but I didn't want to leave you."

Carol knew that was true. They had stayed together, the two of them locked in the safety of their camper. They hadn't even gone out to eat. Carol had thought her husband would eventually leave so he could wrap things up. But instead he had chosen to stay with her, holding her, hugging her, and kissing her.

Carol appreciated that. No matter how much she had enjoyed the extra attention, she couldn't expect him to stay with her again today. Slowly, she nodded. "I knew you would have to talk to Quaid sometime. I was just hoping . . ." She smiled. "Go. The sooner you leave, the sooner you'll get back to me, just please, don't be gone too long."

"I know," he said and reached out and squeezed her hand.

Bronson dropped Carol off at the hotel, then drove to Quaid's office. When he saw Bronson coming, he looked at this watch. "You're late."

"Sorry. Church was longer than I expected." He looked around the cramped office and at Quaid's even more cramped desktop.

Quaid's eyebrows arched. "You went to church?"

"Will wonders ever cease?" Bronson pulled up a chair, placed it by Quaid's desk, and sat down. "That cabin L'ee and Balthasar used to hold my Carol prisoner, know anythin' about it?"

"Belongs to one of our senior citizens. He said a very large lady—we assume that's L'ee—told him she wanted to rent it. She planned to shed all of those extra pounds and the place was ideal because it was so isolated. Benny—that's the cabin's owner—was delighted to rent the place. It's been years since he'd been up there and the extra cash came in handy. He had no idea what was really going on."

Bronson nodded. He hoped the bad experience didn't ruin the idea of using the cabin for future rentals. Benny, like most elderly people, definitely needed the extra income. Bronson took in a deep breath and shook the thought away. "Tell me about Balthasar."

Quaid looked down and squirmed. "He, huh. . . . I'm sorry to say, managed to elude us. You said you wounded him, so I thought surely we'd get him."

Bronson sat up straighter. "You mean he got away?"

"Yeah, but I put out an APB on him. It's just a matter of time." Quaid tapped the tabletop with his fingertips. "You told me you had some information for me."

Bronson got it. Quaid obviously didn't want to talk about Balthasar. That was fine with him. "I do. Have you talked to L'ee yet?"

Once again, Quaid raised his eyebrows. "You haven't heard?"

"Apparently not."

"By the time we reached L'ee at the cabin, she had already slipped into a coma. She passed away this morning and never regained consciousness."

It surprised Bronson that he felt almost a twinge of regret and not just because her death would complicate matters. "Then a lot of what I'm about to tell you can be considered hearsay. Somehow, you, or the Austin police, or the F.B.I.—whomever—will have to find the evidence." Anyone but me, Bronson thought.

"What kind of evidence?"

"Have you heard of Senator Ken Chalmers?"

Quaid hesitated as though afraid to hear where this would lead them. "Of course, who hasn't?"

"There's a dark side to Chalmers that people don't know about." Bronson saw Quaid's eyes narrow in surprise or disbelief, but he didn't say anything. Bronson proceeded to tell Quaid about how the senator had killed Casey Secrist. As Bronson narrated the story, he insisted that his role would be to reveal the details as he knew them. He would not—could not—under any circumstances, get involved in that case.

But deep down, Bronson knew better.

About the Author

L. C. Hayden has penned four mystery novels, including *What Others Know*, the nominee for Left Coast Crime's prestigious Best Mystery Award. She also wrote the WordWright Bestsellers *When Angels Touch You* and *The Drums of Gerald Hurd*. Hayden, who taught for twenty-six years, retired in May 2000. She holds a Master's Degree in Creative Writing from U.T. El Paso. She is member of Sisters in Crime, MWA, Texas Authors Coalition, Mystery Babes, and DorothyL. Besides writing, Hayden enjoys drawing, reading, traveling, and scuba diving. In addition to her novels, Hayden has published over 400 pieces in various magazines.